CHRISTIAN HAYES is the author of *The Glass Book*, *The Fat Detective*, *The Fat Detective in Love* and *The Fat Detective Disappears*. He lives and writes in London.

Also by Christian Hayes

The Glass Book

The Fat Detective
The Fat Detective in Love
The Fat Detective Disappears

CHRISTIAN HAYES

The Fat Detective Disappears

The Fat Detective Disappears

Still Not Based on a True Story

Part One

The Newest Member of the Armchair Detective Society

Chapter One

Bill Sullivan had sellotaped the sign he had printed out at home to the front of the town hall door at the end of the corridor:

The Armchair Detective Society of Kent (and its surrounding areas). Members Only!

By 'Members Only!' he meant that you had to be in possession of a little rectangle of card that he had enlisted his wife to make; her handwriting was neater than his, she could cut straighter than him. She would write the member's name with her fancy fountain pen and he, as President of the Society, would sign it. Mrs. Sullivan would then fill in the field entitled 'Expiry Date' but not until she had yet again debated with him as to why an expiry date was even required. She knew it just meant that she would have to waste more of her time making cards next year.

'What's the point? It's only your friends who show up,' she said.

'That's not true,' said Bill, knowing full well she was right yet again.

His friend Jimmy Finn, who he had known since

school, would show up with a plastic bag of ale bottles, unrefrigerated and clinking, and distribute them to the small gathering of men.

They were all around Bill's age, the youngest being Harry who was seventy and a half. And whenever he failed to bring his membership card with him (which was always), Bill blamed Harry's forgetfulness on his immaturity even though Bill was only four years his senior.

Every week Bill would make sure to check everyone's card and inspected all expiration dates. When Harry failed to present his card yet again Bill was tempted to refuse him entry - someone had to be made an example of, he thought - but he was clutching a second bag of ale and those bottles did allow their evenings to run more smoothly.

'Okay, Harry, I'm letting you in but this is your final warning,' he said. Harry promised to remember his card next time and everyone handed over their £2 entry fee to Jimmy, which, since the use of the town hall room was free, was really just used for the booze.

It was that very same night when Harry was superseded as the youngest member of the Armchair Detective Society of Kent (and its surrounding areas, don't forget). Bill was in the middle of his presentation, entitled *The Complete Short Stories of Cornell Woolrich Part 2, Years 1931 to 1937*, when the door opened and a young woman entered. The whole room turned to her. It was hard for her not to notice the gasps.

Surely she was lost.

Bill quickly instigated his Holmesian powers of deduction. Why would someone who could not be older than twenty - he knew this because that was the exact age of his youngest daughter - be stepping into a room full of male septuagenarians? He thought it highly unlikely that she had any interest in detection and especially in the short stories of Cornell Woolrich. She looked like she kept herself in fine fettle; she was in far better shape than the real ale-sipping group that sat around him. Having made that deduction he could only conclude that she was mistakenly here for the Tuesday night yoga class. Elementary, my dear me, thought Bill.

Bill interrupted his presentation to correct her. 'I'm sorry, yoga class was last night. We have this room booked on Wednesday nights.' He knew Tuesday nights was yoga class because every Wednesday he found discarded yoga mats strewn around the room.

She looked at each of the six faces that were staring at her. Bill, Harry, Colin, Steve, Jimmy and Mick.

'Is this the Armchair Detective Society?' she asked. She knew it was because of the sign on the door.

'Indeed it is,' said Bill, his interest piqued. 'This is the Armchair Detective Society of Kent (and its surrounding areas),' he said, ensuring to recite the title of the society in full, as he always insisted upon.

'Perfect. Then I'm in the right place,' she said, unwrapping her scarf. Bill was baffled. He was sure he could rely on his powers of deduction but he had inexplicably got it wrong.

'A new member,' said Mick to himself, quite astonished.

'Not so fast,' said Bill. There was real excitement from the group that there was a new, youthful member in their midst but Bill was the only one who didn't seem so enthused. 'Are you a member?' It was a pointedly hostile question because everyone knew full well she wasn't.

'No,' she said. 'Is that a problem?'

'Well this is a member's only society, you see...' he said. He was about to launch into his regular treatise on the sanctity of the membership system, one of many standard Bill Sullivan monologues that everyone was all too well aware you could accidentally trigger off if you weren't careful. You then had a hook through your cheek and not even intensive wriggling could get him to shut up but Christina Walker, who she would later introduce herself as, interrupted him, instantly winning the admiration of most of the members of the group.

'Great,' she said, 'where can I get a new member's form?'

Since they had never had a new member they did not have a new member's form. It had never occurred to Bill to create one but he quietly thought it was a sterling idea and was already looking forward to getting home and formatting one on his computer. He would focus on that this weekend, he thought to himself, for a bit of fun.

He liked the way she thought and he warmed to her a little bit.

But the others didn't need any further reason to warm to her. They were already elbowing each other out of the way to be the first to unstack a plastic chair for her from the tower in the corner.

'We're all out of forms,' said Bill, trying to pretend he had a whole stack of them in his drawer at home.

'Next time, then,' she said, taking a seat anyway.

Harry dug into his off-license carrier bag and pulled out a bottle of tepid bitter. He held it out to her. 'No... thank you,' she said. She didn't drink old-man ale which, since she was a twenty-year-old woman, was no real surprise. In fact she didn't drink at all. She preferred to stay alert at all times, she told herself, to be in full control of her senses.

'You can pay up next week, I suppose,' Bill added. 'Now may we continue?'

He didn't wait for an answer and launched back into his ramblings on the writings of Cornell Woolrich. 'In *Murder at the Automat* Woolrich posited a murder mystery in one of the automated American diners that were prevalent in the nineteen-twenties...'

Christina looked around the room. Maybe she'd made a terrible error. What was she doing with all these oldies? They didn't look anything like real detectives.

'...And in *Death in the Air* a bullet shoots through the window of an apartment from a passing train. In *The Earring*, under the pseudonym William Irish, Woolrich shows us a wife quietly returning home from murdering her blackmailer only to find that her earring is missing, surely still glinting at the scene of the crime.'

Bill was interrupted by the sound of a rustling plastic bag as everyone turned to find Harry reaching into the ale supply.

Harry capped off his interruption with a loud cracking-open of the bottle.

'Do you *mind*?' asked Bill. He suspected that Harry only showed up for the beer and had little interest in early American crime fiction.

However, Christina listened attentively - she was surprised how interesting she found it. When President Bill, who had at that point been talking for well over an hour, asked if there were any questions, he had expected the usual silence to drift over the room. But this time the silence was unexpectedly broken. 'How many films were adapted from Woolrich's work?' asked Christina.

Bill reddened. He had no idea.

'I've got that somewhere,' he said, leafing frantically through his notes.

He eventually straightened himself out and, not wanting to look like he didn't know the answer (which he most definitely didn't), announced: 'About two hundred.' He hoped the 'about' would cover any margin of error. When he looked it up later it turned out he had over-estimated by an entire hundred.

He allowed a brief silence to follow his answer before he tried to wind up the evening. 'Well, if there aren't any more questions then that's all until next...'

Christina's hand popped up again. 'I have another question.'

All eyes turned to her.

'Would I be able to present next week?'

'*Present*?' said Bill, a little startled. He hesitated. 'Well... I'm afraid next week is *The Complete Short Stories of Cornell Woolrich, Part 3, Years 1938 to 1942.*'

Harry couldn't take it anymore. He couldn't stand part one, let alone part two - and the idea of a part three was enough for him to renounce his membership. Having someone new speak would be a breath of fresh air. Bill had dominated every evening ever since Giles presented a talk on the non-Holmes stories of Arthur Conan-Doyle - only for Giles to never show up again. (Harry suspected Bill, having seen how well his talk had been received, had made sure to oust Giles from the group.) Harry had been waiting for Bill to get his comeuppance for being such a know-it-all and it had yet to happen. Maybe this would be his chance.

'I say we hold a vote,' and before Bill could protest, he kicked it off. 'All those in favour of letting this young woman present, raise your hand.'

Six arms shot up. Everyone noticed that Bill's had not, but Christina had her own arm right up in the air, her fingers straining towards the ceiling.

Bill had planned to count how many Nos she received but since there weren't any it threw him off and he hesitated a little - his mouth opened but no discernible words came out - before announcing his decision.

'Very well then, you can speak next week... as long as you get your membership all sorted out,' he added.

'I'll make sure she does,' said Harry. He couldn't wait to help her.

'Great,' said Christina, grabbing her scarf. 'I'll see you all next week.'

On the way home Bill realised he had not asked her what she actually would be talking about.

The next Wednesday Bill was surprised to find the room already packed when he arrived, a full fifteen minutes before they were scheduled to start. Everyone was in attendance and a particularly hoppy ale had already been distributed for this special occasion. Jimmy had just opened his second bottle.

Christina was standing at the front, a projector beaming the title slide of a PowerPoint presentation in a square of light onto the wall: 'The Mystery of Eugene Blake'.

Where the hell did she get a projector from? wondered Bill. He didn't want to put a name to the sensation he was feeling. If he did the only word for it would be jealousy.

Christina approached him with her membership card, made out to Christina Walker, and when he held it between his fingers he noticed that it had been laminated, and impressively so. Not even his card was laminated... and he was President! He made a mental note to get his laminated first thing tomorrow.

'Thank you for letting me speak,' she said. Bill barely heard her as he was too distracted by the technical set up and the lamination.

Any signs of her nerves were imperceptible, drowned out by an excitement that had taken over her. She had been working hard on her presentation all week, to the detriment of her English lit coursework, but she didn't want anyone to know how hard she had been working. Instead she wanted it to appear effortless; she wanted the re-writing and endless bedroom-mirror rehearsals to become invisible in the telling.

'May I ask where you got the projector from?'

'I sorted that out,' said Harry, who was sitting within earshot, busily swigging his ale. The extra hoppiness had only served to give him a surge of energy, which was rare of him. He could usually be found comatose on his sofa.

Bill had always assumed that Harry was a luddite of the most primitive order and pictured him in his bungalow writing on a stone tablet. He always thought that Harry would struggle to set the alarm on his bedside FM radio yet here he was hooking up a PC to a projector. He must have borrowed it from that local cricket club that he was always banging on about.

'I hope you like it,' Christina said to Bill.

'I'm sure I'll find it of interest,' he said before taking a seat next to Harry and folding his arms tightly.

Once seven rolled around Christina walked up to the front. Colin got up and snapped off the lights.

The light from the projector was now all that illuminated the room.

'I'm here to talk to you about the Eugene Blake Mystery,' Christina announced.

'A *real* case…' said Bill to himself. His heart raced a little but he actively tried to keep his expression neutral in fear of revealing any excitement to his fellow members.

'I have spent almost a year studying missing person reports,' said Christina. 'I've now seen hundreds, possibly thousands. So that means I've seen thousands of faces…' She brought a face up onto the screen… and another… and another. 'People of all ages, from an eight-year-old boy to a fifteen-year-old girl to a forty-year-old man to a ninety-year-old woman. People are disappearing every day, just turning invisible and falling through the cracks.'

She flicked through the faces, one after the other, each one a stranger looking out at the members of the Armchair Society. One of the faces you would have recognised. It was up there for just a flash but if you had been sitting in that audience there is little chance you would have missed it.

'At the same time as I was collecting these faces I came across this article in the newspaper: "Missing Man Laughs to Death in Barber's Chair".' She showed the article on-screen. It was accompanied by a photograph. 'And I thought to myself that I've seen that face before. So I went back through the faces I had collected.' And she did so in the slides, clicking back through the faces they had just seen until... that face.

'This is Eugene Blake,' she said. She then proceeded to read the article out: '"A stranger, identified as Eugene Blake, was found dead in the chair of a Barbican barbershop around midnight on Wednesday. Previously reported as missing and not seen for several months he died in what the barber described as a laughing fit. The barber was arrested for questioning but has since been released. The funeral will take place on Monday at Gunnersbury Cemetery in West London."

'This is the first sighting of Eugene Blake since his disappearance in November last year. I spoke to a relative of his, his grandmother, who told me she had lost contact with him. He stopped calling. And after a while a stranger was answering his phone and claiming to know nothing about him.

'This case had me so intrigued that I decided to see if I could work out what had happened to him. The first thing to do would be to visit the barbershop where he drew his last breath. And it was that visit which took me on a journey, a journey that led me to this...' She picked up a small leather duffle bag that no one had noticed she had sitting by her feet and placed it on the table. Zipping it open, she took out a series of wirebound notebooks.

'These are the notebooks of Eugene Blake.'

On the table she stacked twelve notebooks, each one identical to the last. She opened one of them and exposed a few of the pages to her audience. 'Each page is full of writing. Page after page. This was clearly a man who had a story he needed to tell. I've come to know these as the Fat Detective diaries because if we open the first one...' She turned one notebook to the first page, '...it is titled "The Fat Detective".' She started to read the first pages: '"My bones were a mess. Imagine a fat man - a really fat man - covered from head to toe in plaster with two sad little eyes peering out..."

'This is the story of how I found these notebooks and what is contained within them...'

Chapter Two

Christina felt that the university library was entirely to blame for her becoming consumed by the mystery of the dead man in the barber's chair.

She was already in her second year of her English literature degree but ever since she had discovered the campus library she found it to be a great distraction from life itself. She had spent hours wandering along the aisles, studying the stacks and pulling out books at random to see what she would come across. She found a turn-of-the-century self-help book called *Memory: How to Develop, Train and Use It*; a novel called *Flatland* in which the main character was a two-dimensional square; and a meticulous history of bookshelves called *The Book on the Bookshelf*. She would find herself there late a night when her fellow students were out partying and doing whatever it was they did (she didn't quite know what that was). She preferred it that way; she could have the whole place to herself.

She always enjoyed the moment the automatic lights turned off above the stacks due to a lack of activity down below. At that point she knew she was truly alone. Sometimes it was only the glow of her little desk lamp that prevented almost total darkness. When it got too dark she would have to stand up and sit down again to trigger the light panel above her head.

She would find time being sucked up by the book in front of her. She would see the words on the page at first but would very quickly see only images, her brain slipping into another zone where words disappeared. The turning of the pages replaced the ticking of the clock and the book itself became some kind of inaccurate papery horological device. Hours would fly by with the turning of those pages.

She would rather stay in the library than go home. Her flatmates did not understand her and after an introductory period of trying to involve her in their activities they had long since given up inviting her. She discovered that if you declined invitations enough times then people would just stop asking.

She had chosen to share a home with these three particular girls because she had found herself becoming friendly with Julie Abbot from her medieval poetry class and in those first few weeks she found herself fantasising about the friendship that could develop between them. She would soon be able to tell her everything, about everything that happened with her sister, and they could talk about books until midnight. She would finally have a best friend like she used to have at school, but just like that friendship, it slowly fizzled out. She suspected she should have made more of an effort but she didn't want to admit to herself that she was the one in the wrong.

She even preferred the library to visiting her own parents. Her sister's disappearance had only served to amplify her parents' personalities. Her father, a meek and unenthusiastic man, became practically mute. A good day for him consisted of a series of monosyllables. Her mother, who had always had little patience for her, now had even less: she used to snap at her for every little thing and now she snapped at her for nothing at all. Her mum had got it into her mind that her younger sister Alicia was the good one, which by process of elimination meant that Christina had to be the bad one.

Her mother saw it as Christina's duty to look after her little sister and so whenever Alicia became upset, which was often, it was seen as Christina's fault. Equally whenever her sister broke something - Alicia was afflicted with the clumsy gene - Christina was to blame. And, years earlier, when Alicia screamed for one of her toys her mother would force Christina to hand it over.

And now that her sister had gone missing Christina was convinced that her mother thought she was to blame. Now when sitting with her mother she was certain that the silence was a result of her mother doing everything she could to prevent herself blurting out accusations of blame.

Christina would now predict how many minutes it would take from stepping through her parents' door to her mother starting an argument. The current record was somewhere around forty-six seconds before conflict arose. Her mother had a knack of burying yet another arrow directly into her heart by criticising one of her insecurities, whether it was her introversion or her insistence on cutting her hair short.

Ever since her sister left they had started to find it more and more insufferable being in the same room as each other. She thought her mother should just grow up.

Her mother also, though she never said it, thought that *she* should grow up.

They had more in common than they thought.

Christina was seriously pissed off at her sister Alicia. Going missing was just the kind of thing she would do and she suspected that the only reason she had disappeared had been to spite her.

She felt as though her sister was holding back her whereabouts just to piss her off. Alicia knew full well where she was and she was just being stubborn by not picking up the phone.

But then again she had always been a very secretive sibling. Whereas other sisters would tell each other everything they would tell each other nothing at all. When they were forced to share a room over the summer of 1997 while Alicia's room was being redecorated (very slowly and shoddily) by their father, she thought that maybe Alicia would open up, but she was presented with silence. She knew that Alicia had some kind of secret other life outside of school hours but she would not reveal any of it to her sister.

She did know about the older boyfriend Alicia had gone out with when she was fifteen and had sworn to keep it secret. It was one of the only sisterly pacts she had ever been offered to enter into and she felt it was her responsibility not to break it. He was way too old for her, Christina thought, but she also felt like she should trust her sister to know what she was doing. But that relationship did not outlive the summer; after a particularly vicious screaming match over the phone their relationship came to an abrupt end.

And that was the last of the sisterly pacts.

The thing is Christina couldn't have instigated a pact

of her own even if she had wanted to. Outside of a boy who came over to platonically watch stupid movies with her (always his choice) she had nothing going on. She daydreamed that when she got to university she would meet mature, erudite, well-read men, but instead all she found were boys who could barely manage personal hygiene let alone intelligent conversations.

She thought about her sister at least once a day and, as ever, wondered where on earth she was and what she was doing at that very moment. Where was her pin on the globe? Alicia had always had a fascination with travel, had memorised all the world's flags when she was a child, and at eighteen had Interrailed around Europe with two of her girlfriends. So in Christina's mind she could be anywhere on the planet right now. Maybe she was at sea or living in a beach hut somewhere. But not knowing was agonising and painful and it had tied a constant knot in her stomach, a ball of fear that had not gone away ever since that fateful night.

In some ways the night she disappeared was entirely unremarkable: her sister just did not come home.

It was as simple as that.

Her mother and father stayed up but around 2 a.m. they all decided to retire to bed. Her sister was almost nineteen at the time and Christina kept reminding her mum, who Christina insisted was prone to overreacting, that, 'She could look after herself'. She assured her that Alicia would be back the next day even though deep down she couldn't be certain. The next night rolled around and her mother clutched the cordless phone in her hand and threatened to call the police. And at midnight, when she couldn't take it anymore, she dialled the number and declared her daughter missing.

All information was logged: when she was last seen, what she had been wearing and whether she had any reason to run away. Her mother insisted that she didn't but Christina wanted to add, 'No reason except for her mother's constant haranguing'. She thought it best in this instance to keep her mouth shut.

Her sister, as the younger, 'prettier' one - defined solely in Christina's eyes by the amount of foundation she was willing to paint onto her face and the hours of hair straightening she was willing to subject herself to (two things Christina had little time for) - her sister now, without being in the room, without possibly even being in the same country, managed to monopolise all her parents' attention. She had upstaged her effortlessly on a grand scale. Her sister would now take up the majority of their parents' thoughts, not leaving much space for Christina at all. *Touché, sister*, she thought. *Touché*.

Christina tried to think the worst. She sat down, closed her eyes, and tried to conjure up the worst possible scenario. She focused on imagining that Alicia was no longer in this world but when she was honest with herself - she challenged herself to be as honest with herself as she possibly could - she was glad to discover that she found such macabre thoughts hard to believe. The more she thought about it the less she believed it and she concluded that Alicia was most certainly alive and well.

Christina almost had admiration for what she had done. Was it selfish? Was it cowardly? Or was it actually brave? She was stepping off the travelator of life and going off to find her fortune. She still owned a small hardback picture book of the Three Little Pigs from when they were kids and that contained an illustration of the three piglets waving their mother goodbye with their trotters. They were off to see the wide world. In Christina's mind this was all that Alicia was doing.

So it was her sister that set her off on her investigation of missing persons. It was an interest borne out of necessity. She wanted to know how many people were found, how long it takes for them to return, and what the reasons were for them to go missing. And it was in the library that she was able to find answers. She was supposed to be studying English but instead she was glued to the Missing Persons' website and also digging out as many books as she could on the subject. She would use her university resources to print out Missing Persons profiles and collect them together in the back of her English file. She lived in constant fear that someone would look at her user account and see just exactly how much paper she had wasted.

When she saw Eugene Blake's face in the morning paper she couldn't help but feel she had seen it before. She went back to her file and flipped through each profile until there he was, staring back at her. And with all the detective fiction she had been reading she had started to see herself as a detective. She thought if she could not solve her sister's case at least she could solve the case of Eugene Blake.

Chapter Three

Night had fallen and Christina had walked through the Barbican and was now standing outside the barbershop. She could see the barber through the large window, busily trimming the hair of a tired-looking office worker. She noted that if Eugene Blake did die here then his death would have been on show for anyone who passed. Quite a spectacle.

As she approached the glass she wondered how she had taken it so far. But she felt that now she had got here there was no turning back. As she stepped inside there was nothing surefooted about what she was doing.

The bell rang above the door and the barber only glanced at Christina before returning to the head he was working on. She looked around the narrow little barbershop with its three gleaming chrome and red leather barbershop chairs, piles of car magazines and stacks of pomade. It looked like it hadn't changed in decades. On the walls were photos of old movie stars: Richard Widmark, Victor Mature, Dean Martin. Elvis looked out at her with his army buzzcut. Presumably a man could point at a photo of Tony Curtis and come out looking just like him.

The barber was holding up a mirror and showing his

customer the back of his head, the place where a patch of baldness had been hidden beneath a thin layer of combed-back, brylcreemed hair.

When the customer had paid up and left the barber grabbed a broom and started to push the discarded hair around the floor.

'You want a haircut?' he asked Christina, not looking at her in the eye. His hair was cut close and under his lip he kept a neatly-trimmed brush moustache.

'No,' she said.

'Good, because I don't cut ladies' hair. Too much trouble for me. Last time I cut a woman's hair she complained so much I didn't hear the end of it. Did you know I can give every man the exact same hair cut? I don't even listen to what they ask for - I just give them a short back and sides and send them packing. They don't even notice. There can't be much inside those heads I cut.' He returned his broom to the corner. 'Now,' he said, 'I expect you are here for some other reason all together.'

'I'd like to ask you some questions,' said Christina.

'About what?'

'About Eugene Blake.'

'I knew it!' he said, throwing up his hands. 'You're not the first person to come in here asking about him. Just last night a very strange man was in here asking questions.'

'Could you tell me what happened?'

'It's all in the article.'

'The article left out a lot of information.'

'You really want to know?' he asked her.

He nodded.

'Okay,' he said. He walked to the door of the

barbershop, twisted the lock and flipped the sign around. He spun the barber's chair and sat facing Christina. 'I had finished for the night and it was late. I was closing up, just doing my final tidying for the day, when I heard a knock on the glass. A frantic knock. And I turned to find this man outside, wet from the rain, desperate to get my attention. I approached the door and I could just about hear that he was asking for me to let him in. He looked like he really needed some help so I opened up for him and he hurried inside.

'"Are you closed?" he asked. He already knew the answer but he walked right in and sat in this very barber's chair. I thought it was strange that someone would be so desperate for a haircut but there must have been a reason for it. And he needed one. He *really* needed one. His hair was all long and scraggy. He looked like he hadn't had a haircut in months and he had this big beard that was overgrown and unkempt. I took pity on him. Maybe he had an important event the next day and this was his last chance to get one. Haircuts are very important to people.

'So as I started to cut his hair, he started to talk. He said he'd been away for a long time and that someone was after him. I asked him who was after him and he said a man called Sarkoff. It was either Sarkoff or Zarkoff, I couldn't quite make it out. He said to me that he was a dead man and he knew he didn't have long. I mean, the guy must have been a lot of trouble. He was talking about himself in the past tense, as though he were already dead.

'And then he started to laugh, as though it were all funny to him. Just a giggle at first and then more of a guffaw, until he was rocking back and forth in my chair and slapping his thigh but then he was laughing so hard that he wasn't making a sound, like the laughter was trapped inside him. Tears started streaming down his cheeks... but then... then he started foaming at the mouth and it wasn't long - it was an instant - that he snapped back into the chair, his eyes wide open, a terrible, twisted grin plastered across his face.

'I didn't know what to do. I had a dead man in my chair. It was pretty terrifying, let me tell you. I called the police and they spent the next hour jabbing me with questions. I told them just what I told you now. They took what must have been a hundred photos of my shop before taking the body away. They took me away for further questioning and I only got out at one a.m. I was back at work at nine. I've never missed a day of work in my life and I'm not going to start just because someone croaked in my chair.'

Christina thanked him for his testimony and as she walked away from that barbershop there had been one word that she had underlined in her notebook: *Zarkoff*.

Whoever this Zarkoff was probably knew something about what had happened to Eugene Blake.

Chapter Four

Christina retreated to the one place where she thought she might be able to find some answers. The next morning she had returned to her university library and she spent a few hours trying to find any reference at all to that strange name.

Thank God he wasn't called Smith.

She first tried the phonebook but where Zarkoff should be she only found Zarda, Zarick and Zarkowski.

She then did a newspaper search, spinning through hundreds of metres of microfiche to no avail.

She then ran a search on all the companies in the UK and came up with only one name: Zarkoff, Inc. And it was there she found an address and this address led to Soho.

She took down an *A-Z* and drew a map for herself, meticulously copying out the journey from Oxford Circus to the address in Soho. And once she had completed it, and even though it was getting dark, she walked straight to the train station.

It took her almost ninety minutes but she found herself heading into the thick of Soho, tracing the path on her hand-drawn map. As she closed in on her target a siren exploded into the air and blue lights lit up the street. A fire engine rushed past her, carrying with it a commotion that only died down once it had disappeared into the distance. Christina did not yet know that both she and the driver of that fire engine had something in common, that they were both heading to the same destination.

Indeed the blue flashing lights reappeared as she turned the corner and found a blaze engulfing the offices of Zarkoff, Inc. Smoke was dancing from its windows and pouring columns into the night sky. There was now no chance of her even getting close let alone anywhere inside. All she could do was stand amongst the crowd of onlookers that had gathered outside and watch it burn.

She marvelled at both the ferocity of the flames and at her sheer bad luck. It was as though someone had known she was coming and didn't want her to get any closer.

Once she had watched the firefighters atop their cherry picker shift their spray from window to window, and once it looked like the fire was close to dwindling, she walked in circles around Soho and felt at a loss. She did not know what her next step would be and she felt foolish for travelling so far away from home. Searching for Zarkoff all day had been exhausting and she hadn't gotten any work on her English essay done which was due in at the end of next week.

She got to bed late that night and her mind was ablaze with images of fire.

She didn't do the reading for her essay the next morning which she had promised herself she would do and when she reached the library she kept walking. She could read on the train instead, she assured herself, but after quickly falling asleep in her seat she found herself pulling into London. And it had barely been twelve hours but she found herself in the light of day standing back in the very spot from where she had watched the building burn. Cordons had since been raised around the building and she walked as close to them as she could. The top two windows were charred and blackened with streaks of darkness fanning out up towards the roof. The ground floor, however, was untouched.

That began a series of visits by Christina to the site that week. She was hoping that the cordons would be removed but they stayed in place. But on Friday a large yellow skip appeared outside. Men were moving in and out of the building dumping burnt and damaged detritus from inside. Mostly it was office paraphernalia: desks, chairs, telephones. Christina installed herself in the cafe across the street at a table that had a perfect view of the building opposite. Over the course of the day she drank several pots of tea and desperately tried to write her essay.

It was only once the cafe was closing, once she had become the last customer in there and the staff were itching to go home, that the workers across the road did the same. They locked the door to the building, piled into their van and drove away.

Christina walked across the street and peered into the skip. Sitting atop the charred chairs and melted phones she saw a box file. It appeared to have been untouched by fire, only dampened by rain. She pulled it out and walked quickly away, not pausing to glance at any of the pedestrians who had clearly seen a young woman rummaging around in a skip.

* * *

She locked the door of her bedroom, placed the box file on her desk and opened the lid. And there it was, sitting on top, staring back at her: the first face.

An identity sheet. It gave the man's name, date of birth and address, and underneath it stated 'Proposed Identity' and there it gave a different name, a different date of birth and a different address. And as she pulled out the pages from the box file she found a whole stack of faces, and then as she looked further, as she leafed through each of them she came across a face she recognised and a name that read: 'Eugene Blake. Proposed name: Stanley Black.'

They gave an address.

She had trouble sleeping that night and found herself awake very early, so much so that she left the house at five thirty and a couple of hours later found herself standing outside a block of flats in East London.

She looked closely at the faces of the men and women who periodically walked out of the block's main entrance. She squinted, trying to recognise the face from the grainy newspaper photograph in the faces of those strangers.

And then one man came out who caught her attention. The more she looked into his face the more she convinced herself she was looking into the face of Stanley Black, otherwise known as our missing protagonist, Eugene Blake.

She followed him to work, which she soon discovered was a butcher's called H. Arthur & Son. She watched him through the window as he got the place set up. She then walked up and down the high street waiting for nine a.m. to tick by. But when it finally did and she pushed the door of the butcher's it was still locked. And the rattle of the door was not enough to get Stanley Black's attention. He was preparing the window display and did not look up from what he was doing.

It had been at least three years since Christina had stepped foot in a butcher's and the sight of the different meats in the window, each one as unappetisingly red as the last, looked to her like a gallery of horrors. She wasn't looking forward to being on the other side of that door.

Stanley Black had laid out the calves' liver, the shin of beef and the oxtail, and was now busy arranging a long string of sausages. She felt a little queasy.

She tapped on the pane in the door and only then did Stanley look up at her. He raised one finger and went back to laying out the final sausages before he removed his gloves and flipped around the 'Closed' sign to 'Open'. He opened the door.

'Hungry?' he asked.

'Aren't you open?'

'We are now,' he said, opening the door fully for her to enter. The full smell of the butcher's hit her in a meaty wave and almost knocked her back. For a split-second she thought twice about stepping inside and entertained the idea of questioning him on the pavement but then she knew if she really wanted to be a detective she couldn't be held back by the sight of blood. She tried not to look too directly at the dark red shadows that were buried deep into the fabric of his apron.

She held her breath and launched herself inside.

'I don't normally get customers busting down our door first thing in the morning,' he said, heading behind the counter. 'What'll it be?'

She momentarily forgot to breath through her mouth and the smell hit her again, the smell of raw meat. She didn't know how to describe it outside of the fact that it was a bloody smell, an icy smell. Somehow it was a red smell. The whole place was red and bloody and icy.

'I'm not going to buy anything. I'm looking for someone.'

'We've got a great deal on sausages today. Four extra if you buy a dozen.' *Sixteen sausages? What the hell would I do with sixteen sausages?*

'Does anyone called Eugene work here?'

'Eugene? No,' he said, shaking his head.

'How about Stanley?'

'You mean Stan?'

'Yes, Stan.'

'You're talking to him.'

'*You're* Stan?'

'I am.'

'I've got a few questions for you.'

'For me?'

'Would you happen to know…'

'I'm sorry, I've really got to finish getting the shop ready,' he said, interrupting her.

'I can wait, I don't mind.'

He could see the disappointment falling across this young woman's face.

'You can come back here if you like.'

'Back where?'

'Behind the counter. I've got some meat prep to do. Just put this on,' he said, handing her an apron, rubber gloves and a hair net. She reluctantly put on all the gear and followed him to the walk-in freezer around the back.

He turned the handle on the heavy door of the walk-in freezer, pulled it open and disappeared inside, leaving Christina teetering on the threshold. She dreaded what she would find in there but what she could see from where she was standing was pretty harmless: cylinders of black pudding stacked on shelves alongside jars of onion chutney.

She took one step inside and instantly regretted it. Hanging from butcher's hooks were an ark's worth of frozen animals: cows, lambs, rabbits, pheasants, pigeons. Stanley had heaved a pig's carcass over his shoulder and was already heading towards her. 'Out the way,' he said, clearly struggling under the weight. She stepped aside and when he turned she found the pig looking directly at her. From the way its mouth was positioned it looked liked it was grinning.

Frozen, she was jolted into action when she saw the door starting to shut. She hurried out to find Stanley standing behind it still hanging onto that pig.

'Man once got locked in one of those,' he said, slamming down the pig on the butchery counter. 'Had to break the lock with a frozen black pudding.'

He picked up a meat cleaver.

'You are not going to… are you?'

'I can't hurt him anymore,' he said. But he spotted something that made him put the cleaver down. 'Damn, the mince,' he said, and rushed over to a small mountain of meat cuts that were stacked up in a tray. He stuffed a few of them into the funnel of a mincer. 'Would you mind?' he asked.

Christina didn't know what he was referring to.

'The handle,' he said.

'Oh,' said Christina, and, almost without thinking,

she stepped in and grabbed hold of it. He piled more meat on top and as she started grinding on the creaking mechanical machine she realised the full horror of what she was doing.

As she cranked, gelatinous pink meat squiggled out of little holes. She had to look away.

'Are you okay?' he asked. 'You're looking a little pale.'

'Yes,' she said. She was a good liar, or so she thought.

'What would a butcher's be without mince? There would be a mutiny,' he said, adding more cuts into the mincer. 'My boss will be here any minute and he'll be really pissed off if this isn't done.'

The crank was stiff and she really had to put her back into it.

'Have you ever heard the name Eugene Blake before?' she asked him.

'Never heard of him.'

'How about Zarkoff?'

'Who is Zarkoff?'

'That's what I'm trying to find out.'

'Are you sure you haven't got me mixed up with someone else?' She was starting to wonder that herself.

'This might be hard to believe but I feel like you might not be who you say you are.'

'I'm sorry?' he asked, frowning.

'I mean… it's not your fault. You can't be expected to know who you used to be.'

'Used to be? I don't follow.'

She lit up a little.

'I've been investigating cases of missing persons and I think you might be one of them.'

'I can't be missing. I'm right here.'

'I don't think Stanley Black is your real name.'

'But it is my name.'

'It's not. Your real name is Eugene Blake. What you know about your whole life is fiction.'

'Why do you keep bringing up that name?'

'Because he's you.'

'How could he be me? I've never heard of him before.'

'You wouldn't have heard it. They make sure of it. They remove every memory you've had of your previous life, even your name.'

'Who does?'

'Zarkoff.'

'How could anyone make you forget your name?'

'I'm not sure, probably some kind of brainwashing.'

'Brainwashing?'

'I don't know how they do it but it must be something like that.'

'And where would this brainwashing take place?'

'I don't know.'

'You don't seem to know very much yet you come here and make these accusations. I don't even know who you are. That's a good question: *who are you*?'

'I'm Christina,' she said. And this was the first time she had ever said it, but she added, as convincingly as she could, 'I'm a private detective.'

He was clearly not convinced.

'A detective? How old are you?'

That question really irked her and she could feel her face flushing red; not through embarrassment but through annoyance. She didn't see what her age had to do with anything.

'I'm *training* to be a private detective,' she said.

'Oh, so I should believe a trainee detective who just shows up and tells me I'm not who I think I am?'

'I *know* it's hard to believe.'

'You're right about that. I'm very sorry to disappoint you but I am the wrong tree to bark up. I think I'll take over from here,' he said, taking the handle from her.

'Look, if you think of anything, please call me,' she said, removing a business card from her pocket and putting it on the side. She had plenty of those left over from a stack she had got printed out last year.

'Don't hold your breath,' he said.

She removed the apron, gloves and hairnet and let herself out.

Walking through the streets the whole encounter replayed relentlessly in her head. Perhaps she shouldn't have revealed so much so soon. Thinking about it she saw how she could have appeared quite mad.

But she had expected that just by saying the name 'Eugene Blake' there would have been at least a glimmer of recognition and when he started to deny any knowledge of that name she thought she would have been able to see through his denial. She thought she would be able to know right away if she had indeed found the missing man. She thought she was good at that kind of thing, thought she was good at reading people, but now that this skill was being tested she was starting to wonder whether she'd ever had what it takes.

She decided to give up several times over the course of that day but a stubbornness inside her kept relighting her determination and that's what resulted in her returning to Stanley's block of flats.

By the time she arrived there it was dark and she

stood under the glow of a streetlamp and wrote down some thoughts in her notebook. She was so involved in scribbling down her ideas that she did not notice Stanley approach her. When she looked up he was only a few feet away.

There was no escape.

'Do you want to come in?' he asked.

'Excuse me?'

'Instead of standing out here in the cold, do you want to come in?' She didn't know how to answer that. All she could come up with was silence. 'First you show up at my work and now you're standing outside my home. You must have something on your mind.'

Everything inside her told her to decline, to make her excuses and leave. She knew it wasn't wise to enter a stranger's flat alone, especially when you had not told anyone where you were or what the hell you were doing.

So, naturally, she said, 'Okay.'

There was a small part of her that thought this was her way in, that this might finally lead to some answers. He seemed harmless, she told herself, and besides, she could take care of herself: she had taken judo lessons for one entire summer. Granted, she was thirteen at the time, but she was sure her muscle memory would kick in if she required it. Failing that, she could always kick him in the balls.

Chapter Five

When she walked into his flat she felt sorry for him. It was just so sparse. There was no ornamentation of any kind: nothing on the walls, no decoration, no personal touches. There was barely any colour.

When she walked into the living room all she found was an armchair, a plastic chair and a rickety coffee table. When she sat down on the chair she realised there wasn't even a TV.

'Would you like a drink?' Stanley asked.

'Please,' she said. He left only to return with a can of lager which he cracked open and passed to her. He cracked another open for himself and sat down on the sofa. Noticing her hesitancy he asked, 'Can I get you a glass?'

'No, this is fine.' She didn't have the heart to tell him that she didn't drink. He took a big slurp and she took a little sip. Nope, beer was still as horrible as she remembered it.

'So why did you feel it was a good use of your day to follow me around? What is it you want to know?'

'I want to know what you can remember.'

'I've had a harder time than people know.'

'You have?'

'I had an accident.'

'What kind of accident…?'

'I don't know the whole story myself.'

'How come?'

'I mean, I can't remember any of it.' He saw just how confused she was. 'I wish I could tell you it was all a blur. At least a blur would be something to go on. This is no memory. Just a gap, a blank. I woke up in a hospital room. No idea how I got there. They asked me what my name was. I said I didn't know. They asked me where I'd come from. I said I didn't know. I mean, that's the kind of thing I *should* know, right?

'When the nurse left the room all I did was think as hard as I could, to try and remember something, *anything*. Eventually they had to tell me who I was.

'They told me my name. Stanley Black. At first it didn't seem to fit but after a few days it started to make more sense. I started to remember *something*, sketches of the past. Not so much scenes or images but words. I could remember my mother's name - Jane Olivia Black - and I could remember my father's - Andrew Henry Black - and I could remember the address of the house where I grew up. I remembered that the dog we used to own was called Pickle. These were undisputed facts.

'They told me I had been found wandering around London with no idea who I was or where I was from. I had been brought into hospital by a concerned member of the public, and once I had been told my name was Stanley Black I at least knew who I was. I had my identity back.

'When they discharged me they told me my address. They had found it in my coat pocket when I was brought in. To me my address was, like my name, nothing but another undisputed fact. They gave me my belongings which included a key and when I reached the address, this little flat on this concrete estate, the key fit the lock.

'But it was alien to me. There were clothes in the wardrobe and dishes in the kitchen cupboard but there was no evidence of me ever having lived here. It was sparsely furnished with furniture that was entirely void of personality. There was not a single picture on the wall. There were no objects: no stereo, no tapes, not a single book. It was like I had never lived here but I must have done. I had the key in my hand. And I sat in this living room that first night in total silence and I did not feel any sense of having come home. I felt like I was sitting in the flat of a complete stranger.

'But I've come to understand that it's all the result of my accident: it's as though it wiped me out and I had to start afresh. The clothes I found in the wardrobe didn't fit me. I had never seen them before. I had to go out the next day with the very little money I had and buy something I could actually wear. It took me a few weeks but that sense of home slowly arrived until it felt like I had been here for years.

'The money ran out pretty quickly and I had to get a job. When I saw the local butcher's was hiring I took a position there and he didn't mind training me up. It's only been a few months but he's already given me a lot of responsibility. I must say I was very surprised,' he said, interrupting himself.

'About what?'

'Surprised when you showed up at work this morning and were so eager to ask me all those questions. I was certain you must have got the wrong guy. That was until…'

'Until?'

'Until you said the name Eugene Blake.'

'So you do know who Eugene Blake actually is?'

'Not quite. But when you said that name it rang a bell at least. I had to think twice as to where I had come across it, and then I remembered.' Stanley got up from his chair and left the room. When he returned he was holding a small leather duffle bag. 'When I left the hospital they only gave me one possession.' He laid the bag on the coffee table and unzipped it. When he pulled it open Christina saw that it was filled with notebooks. As he took them out she counted twelve A4 wirebound notebooks, each one identical to the last.

'What are these?' she asked, picking one up.

'They must have got me mixed up with someone else. It's some kind of story and I'm sure whoever it is who wrote it is looking everywhere for these. But look here,' he said, opening one of the notebooks. On the first page was a name written in blue ink: Eugene Blake.

She flicked through one of the books. Every line on every page was filled with handwriting.

'Did you tell the hospital they weren't yours?'

'I did but they insisted they belonged to me.'

Her eyes passed over the first sentence in the notebook she was holding: 'My bones were a mess. Imagine a fat man - a really fat man - covered from head to toe in plaster with two sad little eyes peering out…'

He could see the interest it had sparked in her.

'You want them?' he asked.

'I couldn't take them from you.'

'Take them, I insist.'

'Well I'd like to read them, at least. Have you read them?'

'I tried but I struggled to get through even the first one. The story is a bit too convoluted. I prefer things with a bit more realism.'

'Well I would certainly like to borrow them.'

'Take them,' he said, packing them back in the bag and zipping it shut.

Christina had entered with nothing and found herself leaving with a treasure trove. She was certain these pages would reveal what happened to Eugene Blake.

Chapter Six

Christina locked her bedroom door, unzipped the bag and laid the notebooks out on her carpet. She discovered that some of the notebooks were numbered. She looked through them until she found a number 1 written on the first page.

Lit only by the light of her bedside table lamp she opened the notebook.

What Christina proceeded to read were some very strange stories. They told the story of how a bored, overweight office worker posted an ad on the world wide web offering his services as a private detective - *Private Detective For Hire, No Case Too Small* - and found himself with a missing person's case. She read how a woman called Melissa White had invited him to her house and told him how her husband was missing. He accepted the case without having any prior training or knowledge about what he was doing. Christina found the story intriguing - engaging even - but found it very hard to believe. Rather than a journal or diary it read like fiction. There were too many plot holes, too many half-sketched characters. The whole story didn't add up. Was she reading the work of some kind of fantasist, someone who believed it all to be true or, on the other hand, someone who knew it all to be fiction?

By the time she reached the conclusion of that first story it was two a.m. and she had reached notebook number four. She was so intrigued by the whole thing that she continued onto notebook number five and read about how Eugene Blake got involved with the Brotherhood of Broken Hearts, a network of pick-up artists who scoured the streets of London searching for women. It also told the story of how he took on the case of a neighbour's husband and followed him around London to discover that he was leading a double life. But this story did not really conclude. Instead Eugene Blake just disappeared. 'I have to interrupt the book here to let you know that I cannot find him. I have looked everywhere. I have to report to you that Eugene H. Blake has gone missing...' It was not clear who wrote those final words.

The following pages of that notebook were blank.

It was close to five now but she was not tired. The stories had set her mind racing and she felt strangely alert.

She got up from her bed and looked for the next numbered notebook in the sequence. She had just completed reading notebook number eight but she found that the final notebooks were not numbered. How was she to know which sequence they should go in? She decided to choose one at random and see whether it gave her any answers at all.

Part 2

The Eugene Blake Notebooks

Chapter Seven

Have you ever been beaten up? I mean, *really* beaten up?

What surprised me was just how concrete Maxwell's fists felt as they crashed against my jaw, my cheekbone and my nose. They did not seem to be made of flesh and bone but of something much harder; in my blurred mind I saw fists of stone. He knocked all thoughts out of my brain except for one: I just wanted to survive the onslaught. It's amazing how violence focuses the mind. But it wasn't like I could fight back; I was already on the floor with my hands up to my face. And then his boot came into the equation, his toe swinging hard into my stomach and knocking all the wind out of me. And I don't know if I was then knocked out by a particular blow to the head or if the sheer pain was enough to cause me to pass out.

When I came to I found myself on the floor of my flat, illuminated by the light streaming from the corridor through my front door. The pain seized me instantaneously, pulsated inside my stomach and burned across my face. The first thing I did was turn my head to see if Maxwell was still there but there was no sign of him. Emily had also disappeared. That would be the last I would ever see of her.

The bruises on my arms and back made themselves known as I untangled my body from that floor, straightened myself out and got to my feet.

I did not wait a moment. I walked into my bedroom, took out a small leather duffle bag from my wardrobe and stuffed it with a few clothes. I then retrieved a screwdriver and proceeded to unscrew the panel from the side of my bath. And from inside the under-tub cavity I pulled out that briefcase.

I locked the door of my flat and dropped the key into my pocket. At that time I did not know just how long it would be until I returned.

Rather than finding darkness outside I found the earliest signs of dawn. That sky revealed that I had been out cold far longer than I had thought.

I installed myself in a tube station cafe when it opened at five-thirty and drank coffee until I couldn't stand it any more. I could see the staff whispering conspiratorially and glancing over at me. They must have been looking at my face but I avoided my reflection. I didn't want to see how bad I looked.

At nine I walked into my bank as soon as they opened but the manager who opened the door stopped me.

'Are you alright?' he asked.

'I'm fine,' I said, but the pain that pulsated through my body suggested otherwise.

The bank teller behind the glass was equally horrified and I even saw her hand shaking a little as she tapped numbers into her computer. She didn't ask any questions, just emptied out my bank account - every penny I had in the world - and handed it to me stack by stack as I stuffed the notes into my bag. I walked out of there with a big fat zero stamped on my bank account.

I walked into Soho and found the address. I was not there for very long and found myself back on the street but now without the briefcase.

I spent the day wandering the streets of Soho. The soles of my feet were aching and the hunger that crept up through me drained my energy further. And it was as night fell, as the shadows of Soho stretched out and took over every corner, that I noticed the eyes, the eyes staring out at me. Not directly though - I could never catch anyone looking directly - but I knew that just before my head had turned they had been looking, staring at this destitute and beaten-up man who had been rejected by the city. And each street I would turn down I would find that every head turned away as I tried to catch them staring. And they muttered under their breath, I'm sure they did, but I could never make out what they were saying. And then the buildings themselves started to close in on me, and that was what drove me out of there, what pushed me towards the station and before I knew it I was on a train around midnight with London disappearing into the distance.

I drifted in and out of sleep, or maybe in and out of consciousness. My guts hurt, my head hurt. I just wanted to lie down.

I was awoken by the conductor.

'Are you okay?' I could see fear in his face. 'What the hell happened to you?'

I looked at my face in the dark reflection. It did not look good.

'You need to see a doctor,' he said.

The train was no longer moving. I grabbed my bag, dodged the conductor and stumbled off the train. He watched me through the glass as I passed the carriage window and walked along the platform.

As I limped away from the station I could hear the sound of seagulls in the metallic morning sky. I walked until I found myself standing by the seafront of a run-down seaside town. I explored the buildings along the promenade: fish and chip shops, ice cream parlours, and amusement arcades, each one of them shuttered.

The sea was blue-black and inky and my shoes sunk into the sand. I impressed a series of footprints that led towards the breaking waves and stood at the very edge of where they unrolled themselves. I let the grains settle themselves in the dotted holes of my brogues.

I sat against the stone wall that led up to the seafront and closed my eyes for just for a moment. It felt good to feel the breeze against my burning skin and the soft sand beneath my body. I listened to the sound of drifting waves. They must have contained a lullaby because they dragged me to sleep.

I woke up under a brighter sky to the sight of a small, sandy dog peering at me, tongue hanging out. Its owner called the dog away from me and it obediently returned, peppering paw prints into the sand. It was meant to be fetching a tennis ball but it had become distracted by the washed-up man on the beach. It had tried to fetch me instead.

I looked down and saw just how much sand had gathered in the crevices of my clothes. I must have twisted and turned through the sand in my sleep. There were now a few early morning faces on the beach looking towards me and I realised I must have been looking like a shipwrecked castaway who had appeared overnight.

I got myself up, walked up the steps to the promenade and dumped the sand out of my shoes. As I headed away from the beach I saw a town slowly whirring into motion: chairs were being unstacked, streets were being cleaned and buses were sleepily dragging themselves along the road.

I passed some dreary office buildings and came across an entire block that had been bordered up. I peered through the gap in the fencing only to find eyes staring back at me: the eyes of an old carousel horse. Once gilded, the carousel and all its horses had long since faded.

I walked around the corner and found a gap in the fencing that I just about managed to squeeze myself through.

When I emerged on the other side I found a ghostly amusement park stretch out before me. I walked around the old big dipper: a tall, winding wooden structure with slats missing like absent teeth. Weeds had overtaken it, winding up its beams and creeping through every crack they could find, and its carriage sat rusted and waterlogged at its lowermost dip.

There was a shooting gallery and only one of the air rifles remained, the others having been severed and removed. The display shelves were now barren of prizes. The cushioned mallets of the whack-a-mole kiosk hung down, the leather split, their foam creeping out. Amateurishly painted images of Daffy Duck and Goofy adorned the kiosks.

The sound of creaking drew my eyes up to the swing ride seats swaying slowly in the sea breeze above my head. Once full of life, the park had been left to deteriorate and face the elements.

It had started to rain so I sat inside a Waltzer carriage as though waiting for the ride to begin. When I found I couldn't keep my eyes open any longer I lay down on the seat of the carriage and re-entered the dreams that had been interrupted by that sandy little canine.

Chapter Eight

I looked at my reflection in the back of a spoon. That warped little reflection made my face look even worse.

I had to find somewhere to stay. I couldn't spend another night in the Waltzer carriage.

'Do you know any decent hotels around here?' I asked the waitress once she'd brought my coffee.

'You can't move for B&Bs around here. Just throw a stone and you'll hit one.'

And she was right. Only a few doors down, on the seafront, I found a 'Rooms Available' sign on the door of a B&B called The Palace. There was nothing palatial about it; it was a run-down, narrow little building that seemed to be shrinking with age. At least I would get a view of the sea, I thought.

I walked up the steps to the front door, rang the bell and waited.

When the door opened a woman with green curlers in her hair stared out at me.

'Yes?' she asked.

'Do you have any rooms free?'

She looked me up and down. 'Where's your luggage?'

'Here's my luggage,' I said, holding up my little

leather duffle bag.

'Where's your suitcase?'

'I don't have a suitcase.'

'Then we don't have any rooms.'

'But it says right here that you do,' I said, pointing to the sign which now stood between us, blu-tacked to the pane in the open door.

'I have a rule that says to be wary of a man who comes knocking without a suitcase.'

'I'm just here for tonight.' That wasn't entirely true. I didn't actually know how long I would be there for.

'Just tonight? You're not on the run, are you?'

'You get many people on the run here?' I was becoming a little insolent as I grew tired of standing out in the cold.

'You'd be surprised how many people are running away from something. You've come down from London?'

'Yeah.'

'There we go then. It's always the guys from London who are running away from something. In one guest's room we found stolen jewels, in another a shotgun. Your face is a right giveaway, it tells me you've been in trouble.'

I looked in the reflection of the open door. She was right.

'Just a little boxing, that's all.'

'You? Boxing? You don't look like a boxer.' It had meant to be a quip but she had taken it seriously.

'I'm in the over-weight category.'

'Well I don't want any fighting around here.'

'Just one night and I'll be gone.' It was getting late and I really didn't want to return to that theme park.

She gave me one final look up and down and I watched her read me from my scuffed-up shoes to my beat-up face.

'Okay, one night. But you pay now.'

'No problem,' I said, unzipping my bag.

As I signed myself into the registration book she said, 'I expect you'll be wanting a fry-up tomorrow.' I was slightly offended that she would assume, just because of my size, that I would be wanting a fry-up.

'Yes,' I said. 'I would.' She just so happened to have assumed correctly.

'Breakfast's at seven,' she said.

'Until when?'

'Until never. Breakfast's at seven.'

'It's just that it's usually until nine, ten, something like that.'

'I'm not hanging around for three hours waiting for you to come down just so I can make you breakfast. *I've* got things to do.' She dragged the cash off the table and counted it up before shoving a key in my hand.

'Second floor. No smoking, no pets,' she said. It's not like I had a puppy hiding in my raincoat.

I walked up the stairs and she watched me every step of the way.

When I pushed open the door of my room it was dark inside. When I dragged the curtains across I found that the room did not look out towards the sea but towards a car park. How picturesque.

When I sat on the bed dust bounced into the air. The room felt like it hadn't been slept in for weeks. Dust was a theme; it was everywhere.

I clicked the light off, turned on the little radio on the bedside table and lay down on the bed. I thought it would be best to sleep on top of the duvet rather than submit myself to an experiment in hygiene by sliding inside, and I soon fell asleep to the sounds of the shipping forecast. *South Biscay. Southeast FitzRoy. Southwesterly veering westerly, five or six, occasionally seven in north. Occasional rain. Good. Occasionally poor.*

I was a long way from home and I didn't know when I was ever going to return.

Chapter Nine

I met her down on the beach only a few days later. I'd seen her from afar and found myself approaching, more out of curiosity than anything else. Up close she had very expressive eyes, dark and glassy, and if you looked closely into them you could see the entire beach reflected back at you. She was soft as clouds when you ran your hand over her.

I was introduced to her by Jake, her handler.

'This is Tabatha.' She was an overcast grey. Oatey, his other donkey, was mouse-brown.

He told me he needed a hand, that he couldn't take care of two donkeys at once. If we were to team up it would be twice the money. By that point I was getting low on funds so I asked exactly what I would need to do.

'It's easy,' he said.

The first customer of the day had approached us, a small girl and her mother.

'How much is it?' asked the girl's mum.

'Just three quid,' he said. 'Eugene here will be walking Tabatha today,' he told her.

'I will?'

'It's easy,' he said quietly to me.

He lifted the girl up, plonked her in the saddle and handed me the reins. 'Just walk her up as far as the bandstand, then circle around and walk her back again.'

The girl looked excited to get going; Tabatha looked like she didn't care one way or the other. But when I took a step forward and tightened the reins I realised that Tabatha did care. She did not move an inch and was clearly in no mood to go walking today. I tried again, pulling hard, digging my feet into the sand and leaning forward with all my weight but Tabatha made sticking to one spot seem effortless.

When she curled her head round to Jake and looked him in the eye I got a sense that she missed being walked by him and was not so enthused by this fat stranger who was trying to take her away.

The little girl started to laugh at me.

'Is anything wrong?' the mother asked Jake, looking a little concerned.

'No, nothing's wrong. It's just his first day, that's all,' he said, walking up to me and speaking conspiratorially. 'She's a stubborn little thing. You've just got to walk confidently, show her who's boss. A short, sharp tug ought to do it.'

I stepped forward and gave the reins a tight snap. My efforts were enough to make her take one step. Then another. Then another. And soon enough Tabatha was stepping slowly along the sand and behind us we left a trail of my shoe prints and her hooves.

Her stubbornness had been a little test but now that she was in motion she took it all in her stride. She didn't mind me walking her and she didn't even mind the girl who was bouncing on top of her and tugging on her ears.

I soon learned that Tabatha was a peaceful creature, a calm animal in a perplexing, chaotic world. And as we walked alongside the drifting waves I felt that she was getting to like me.

She clearly new the drill; when we reached the bandstand she circled round without any instruction from me and walked back towards Jake and the girl's mother.

'Good job,' said Jake. He lifted the girl off. 'Not bad for your first go,' he said once the girl and her mother had left. 'Make sure to go as slowly as you can to make it last longer and always remember to take the money first. And keep the kids away from the back of her. She can get a bit kicky.' I found that hard to believe.

A boy and his mother had approached and were waiting to get on.

'I'm sorry, love. He's too big,' Jake said, pointing to the large boy in dungarees.

'Too big? That's outrageous,' said the mother.

'He'd squash her.' He had a point. The boy was huge. 'How old is he?'

'Seven.'

'Seven? He looks twelve! What are you feeding him?'

She grabbed his hand. 'Come on Eric, away from the rude man!'

Even though Jake would often turn business away for whatever reason took his fancy, Tabatha proved a hit and that day I took over forty kids out for rides.

I was out in the sun for so long that day that the next day I woke to find that my neck and face had turned a bright shade of red. From that point on I slathered my face in sun tan lotion and wore a floppy-brimmed hat that I bought from a tourist kiosk.

I spent my evenings taking care of Tabatha in the stables, feeding and grooming her. I had certain tasks to fulfil which all fell under my remit and I would top up her trough with hay and replenish her bucket with water. Once a day I'd also give her a portion of grain which she seemed to particularly enjoy sticking her nose into.

After a few days I bought some carrots from the supermarket and sat next to Tabatha peeling them so that she wouldn't have to eat the skin. And we'd sit there, me and my donkey, sharing carrots. As a treat I would give her a few polo mints. She must have had the freshest breath in the country (for a donkey).

I'd comb her fur in circular motions with a currycomb; for her tail I would use a ladies' hairbrush.

The more time I spent with her the more I felt she came to understand me. It was as though she liked my company and enjoyed our conversations. Yes, I talked to her and she listened intently.

The money I made with the donkey allowed me to keep paying for the room at the B&B and for the next six months that suited me fine. I grew to like the routine of it all and soon I forgot all about my old life back in London.

It was a shock that did it, a shock in black and white that meant I would have to return and face up to my past.

Chapter Ten

The greasy spoon I visited every day hadn't been touched since the sixties. Rectangular formica tables jutted out from the walls and the original leather upholstery had long since worn away; in the back pinball machines sat unlit and unplayed. Even the waitress hadn't been touched since the sixties: she wore plastic cat eye specs and kept a spare pencil in her beehive. And the other patrons were museum pieces, antiques from another time: lone men and women who looked lost as they gazed out to sea through the window and made their way through their choice of artery-clogging meals.

A chalkboard had the special of the day scrawled across it. Today's was jellied eels and chips.

The food itself looked like it had come from a greasy spoon museum: two rubbery eggs, shrivelled sausages, a crowd of beans and a sweaty slice of bacon.

I added as much milk as I could to the coffee but it stubbornly stayed black.

I ripped through the egg, setting yolk spilling across the plate, tore into the sausage and jammed it into my mouth before turning the page of the newspaper I had laid out on the table. That's when I saw it: my own face staring back at me in newsprint black and white.

The headline read:

Missing Man Laughs to Death in Barber's Chair

I knocked my coffee across the page.

'Is everything okay?' asked the waitress who had seen the coffee spill and was now trying to soak it up with a dishcloth.

I was unable to answer. I was too busy trying to read the sopping, caffeinated article that was now draped over my fingers.

A stranger, identified as Eugene Blake, was found dead in the chair of a Barbican barbershop around midnight on Wednesday. Previously reported as missing and not seen for several months he died in what the barber described as a laughing fit. The barber was arrested for questioning but has since been released. The funeral will take place on Monday at Gunnersbury Cemetery in West London.

'I'm dead,' I said. She looked at me funny.

'Excuse me?'

'I'm dead,' I repeated. I paid up and left my food uneaten.

Walking down the street I felt a deathly sensation, as though the article had revealed something to me that I already knew to be true: that I had somehow died a long time ago, an event so imperceptible that I had barely noticed. And only then did I realise just how the lonely streets of that little seaside town paid no attention to me. I walked down to the sea and failed to make an impression on the sand; the waves drifted on regardless.

Chapter Eleven

My host put the breakfast down on the table as she always had. It was the same every morning: two fried eggs on toast, and every morning the toast was burnt. I could hear her scraping the carbon into the sink as I made my way down the stairs.

Her name was Jeanette and she would sit with me over breakfast. She seemed to like to watch me appreciate her cooking. At first she was suspicious of me but now, six months later, I appeared to keep her company. That's why when I finished my breakfast that morning it was a little hard to tell her what I had to say.

'I've packed in the job,' I said.

'Packed it in?' she said. 'Whatever for? You liked that job. I told all my friends about you: the donkey man walking up and down the beach. They look out for you, you know.' I know they did. They liked to wave, too, and wouldn't stop waving until I waved back. If I didn't return the gesture I feared they would stand there waving until the sun went down.

'Something's come up.'

'*Something*?'

'Back in London.'

'What do you want to go back there for? It'll only

make you miserable. You said so yourself.' She looked a little hurt. 'Where am I going to get another guest from?' Guests were indeed sparse in that little B&B. In all my months there there were only nine other guests that passed through. She would often forget to put the vacancy sign in the window and I ended up doing it for her. But she was so suspicious of anyone who stepped foot over her threshold that she would often send away potential customers. I think ultimately she had a phobia of strangers in her home. She was really in the wrong business. When her husband died she should have packed it in.

'I think it's time to go back home. I can't hide out here my whole life. Even an ostrich has to pull its head out of the sand sometimes.'

I felt like she was going to miss me and as I ate my eggs I tried to remember who the last person was who missed me but I concluded that there was not a single person out there wondering where I was. I knew that I never showed up in anyone's thoughts, let alone in their dreams.

'I'll come visit,' I said.

'That's just what my daughter said. Well, tonight we will have a final meal, a final celebratory send off. I'll make you a nice steak. I'll pick one up later from the butcher. I'll even put an egg on it.'

'I'm afraid what I've got to do is urgent and cannot wait. I've got to go right now. I'll write to you, I promise.'

'Everyone says that and they never do. I haven't received a letter in years.'

She picked up my empty plate and walked back to the kitchen. I walked up those creaky steps one last time to get my bag and when I came down again she refused to come out of the kitchen.

'All right, bye then,' she said, coldly.

'Here's a bit extra,' I said, holding out some money.

'Okay, thanks,' she said, not making eye contact with me at all and not taking the notes. I just left them, along with my keys, on the hall table and shut the front door after me. Rather than seeing it as though I were leaving the B&B she saw it as though I were leaving her. I took one final look at the front of that tired hotel and walked off down the promenade.

With my suitcase in hand I went to say goodbye to Tabatha but once I told her I was leaving she didn't seem to be in the best mood either.

'I have to go, Tabatha, but I'll come visit you.' I couldn't exactly write to her too.

She looked away and went back to burying her nose in the straw bucket.

I thought I would groom her one last time but as I was brushing her tail she kicked me and I flew right out the door.

I'm sure she didn't mean anything by it.

Chapter Twelve

It was late and the street was lit only by the glow emanating from the narrow barbershop with its red and white candy stick still spinning outside. I could see the barber inside, eating a ham sandwich and dropping crumbs on the evening edition he was reading.

I pushed the door open.

The barber looked up from his paper and over his glasses.

'We're closed,' he said.

'The sign says you're still open.' He looked up at the clock on the wall. 'I've really got to remember to flip that sign over. Fine. I'll fit you in,' he said, getting up and folding up his newspaper. 'Take a seat.'

I took my raincoat off and sat down in the barber's chair, all gleaming chrome and red leather.

He draped a sheet around me, fastened it at my neck.

'What'll it be?' he asked.

'Just a trim,' I said.

He sprayed my head with water.

'I've cut thousands of heads in my time and it's always a trim. Why's it always got to be a trim?' He held the comb and scissors in one hand and began combing back my hair. He began to tut. 'Dear, dear. Do you know you're going thin back here?' Of course I knew. I knew all too well. '*Very* thin.'

'What can I do about it?' I asked.

It was a serious question and I was hoping for a serious answer.

'If I knew I'd be a millionaire.' That answer was no help at all. I could see he wasn't afflicted with any thinning at all. Somewhere over sixty, he had a miraculously-full head of gleaming white hair. Maybe he *did* know the secret, perhaps an elixir that you are only given once you are accepted into the elusive Barber's Circle. Come to think of it, have you ever seen a bald barber?

I glanced at him, tried to discern whether he was distracted in any way. But there was no sign of anything out of the ordinary, no sign that only a few days earlier a dead man had been sitting in the very chair I was now sitting in.

'Do you normally work this late?'

'Only when I don't feel like going home.'

'Why wouldn't you feel like going home?'

'I'm in the doghouse at the moment. I know the minute I step back through the door tonight my wife will start haranguing me so I just tell her I have to work late and I can get some peace and quiet. I can listen to the radio and read the papers. I've got a little microwave in the back. And I can always have a little beer here too without being hassled about it. Sometimes you just need a drink after work. I once came home to find her cracking open my cans and glugging them down the sink. Heartless. Totally heartless.'

He was snipping away with those scissors which made a pleasant slicing sound as the blades slid together.

'You had someone come in a few days ago... and something happened to him...' His clipping stopped.

'Not another one.'

'Another what?'

'I knew I shouldn't have talked to that newspaper.'

'Why not?'

He started snipping away again.

'Every day now... every day since it was printed I've had someone come in here and ask me about it. There really are some sick people out there. Such morbid fascination.'

'I must say I have more of a reason to be interested...'

'Why's that then?'

'Because my name is Eugene Blake.'

'You're joking.'

'No, it really is my name.'

'Well,' he said, continuing to cut my hair, 'that really is a coincidence. Must have been pretty funny having your name in the papers like that, telling you you're dead. I had my name in the papers and I didn't like it, but at least I'm not the one who croaked. I know they're saying the case is all closed and all that but don't you think it suspicious?'

'Suspicious how?'

'I mean, a guy taps on my window late at night and does everything he can to convince me to let him in. I tell him I'm closed but he was in some kind of distress. He really seemed to want this haircut so I let him in. I tried to make chit-chat with him, just some small talk, but he started telling me that he had been poisoned and that he didn't have long to live.'

'Poisoned?'

'That's the part I didn't tell the papers. I asked him who poisoned him, and he told me it was some guy named Zarkoff.' And he told me how he had started to laugh, how he went all mad in the chair, and then how he suddenly stopped laughing.

As he had been telling me the story he had been snipping away. Once he had finished I found him combing it back as tightly as he could and dipping his hand into a pot of clay and dragging it over my head. By the time he was done everything was glazed stiff, and the clay only proceeded to make it appear thinner than it actually was. Without notice he started to lather my face and almost before I knew what was going on he had a cutthroat razor in his hand and with a few flicks of the wrist he had shaved my week-old beard off entirely and made my moustache pencil thin. Once he had got rid of the shaving foam I stared at myself in the mirror and looked back at myself with a pencil-thin moustache and slicked-back hair. I looked like one of the movie gangsters he had framed up on his wall.

Chapter Thirteen

Before heading home I made a detour. I picked out some tulips - I'd always liked those - and I thought my corpse, looking up through the soil, would appreciate the gesture. As I stood in the queue to pay I thought about how the phrase 'it's your funeral' was literally true in this case. The guy behind the counter rang up the flowers.

If only he knew who those flowers were for. 'I was buried this morning,' I said to him. He looked at me, then continued on as if I hadn't said anything. In fact he looked a little annoyed. He didn't say a single word to me and when he handed over the flowers he didn't ask if I wanted a receipt.

The cemetery was situated alongside an A-road and I pictured my coffin rattling around in the back of the hearse as it raced along at sixty miles an hour.

The sky had darkened as I stepped through the cemetery gates, flowers in hand, and while it was somewhat more peaceful inside than out on the road I could still hear the rush of traffic from beyond its walls.

There was hardly anyone around, just the silhouettes in the distance that seemed to drift past the graves. In this deep twilight they made convincing impressions of ghosts.

I wound a path through the cemetery and glanced at the names on the gravestones I passed: Juliet Daniels, Michael Nichols and Eric Jones, but all these graves had been there for some time. I was looking for a fresh plot, a new burial with a clean headstone and I kept going, blindly tracing my way along the labyrinthine pathways that branched out in all different directions.

Up ahead I saw a woman standing solemnly in front of a gravestone. I tried to pass quietly so as not to disturb her private moment of contemplation. She was smartly dressed in a long dark-grey coat and only as I got closer did I notice that she was sniffing away tears. But only when I looked down at the gravestone did I see the words:

Here lies Eugene Blake.

The stranger caught my eye. 'Did you know Eugene?' she asked, a question that she had managed to saturate with hope. I nodded, too shocked to speak. All I could do was lay my flowers down next to hers on the gravestone, yellow touching red, with a solemnity that made it feel like I really was laying flowers on my own grave.

She seemed genuinely concerned about me and I could only conclude that I had done little to hide the distress from my face.

'Are you okay?' she asked.

'It's just all so sudden,' I said. I was finding it hard to process a grave with my name on it.

'You're right, it was just so sudden. Did you know him well?' she asked.

'Pretty well,' I said. If she only knew.

'I didn't see you at the funeral.'

'I didn't hear about what had happened to him until it was too late.'

'It must have come as quite a shock to you.'

'Oh it did, believe me.'

'Were you close?'

'You could say that.'

'My name is Heather by the way, Heather Blake.'

Blake?

'Do you know what happened to him?'

'All I know is he disappeared, just one day didn't come home. And then eight weeks later they found him in that barbershop chair.'

'Was he in any trouble?'

'Not that I know of.'

'And did you know him well?'

'We were engaged.'

'*Engaged*?'

'Yes. He proposed only three months ago.'

'How long did you know him for?'

'Not long. I met him only six months ago. You could say it was a whirlwind romance but it was the best six months of my life.'

I read the gravestone. *Hang on*, I said to myself. 'Loving Father and Partner'?

'I didn't know he was a father.'

'Well, he will be... or should I say, would have been in about five months.'

'Oh...' I said. Only then did I notice the bump.

'So you... and him...?'

'I arranged the headstone. There was no one else. He didn't have any family.'

As she walked ahead I took a final moment to look down at the marble and wondered: Who the hell was buried in my grave?

It had started raining heavily and Heather was stepping quickly along the pavement but she hadn't quite managed to shake me. I was close behind. I thought we were both taking the long walk back to the station but she stuck out her arm and a cab that had been heading towards her stopped. She opened the door, perched one foot on its threshold and turned to me.

'There's no point you walking in the rain. Get in,' she ordered.

I didn't argue with her and stepped off the wet pavement and into the cab.

As we rode together in silence into the suburbs she glanced at me from time to time. This culminated in a particularly long stare.

'Why do you look familiar to me?' she asked.

'I do?'

'You're sure we haven't met before?'

'Positive,' I said.

The cab pulled up outside her house and she got out, leaving me to settle the fare.

As the taxi pulled away I made a note of her house number but when she got to the door she turned. 'You'd better come in,' she said. That was easy. At least now I wouldn't have to break in.

I could feel the rain penetrating my shoes and soaking my socks. 'I'd better,' I said.

As soon as she opened the front door a light ginger cat circled around her boots. 'Get away from me, Lotte,' she said, putting her soaking bag down and trying to tug her coat off. The cat figure eighted around her feet. 'Lotte, away!'

The hallway had been laid with a spotless carpet and I balanced myself on one leg, flamingo-like, and struggled to pull off my muddy shoes. And once they were off I realised I was standing on her welcome mat in mismatched socks.

'You'd better take them off,' she said.

'Off?'

'Your socks. They're soaking. Put them on the radiator.'

I did what she said: I peeled them off and hung them on the radiator.

Now I looked down and saw the sad sight of my feet on her carpet. I curled my toes so that she wouldn't have to lay her eyes on my ten little monstrosities.

The ginger cat miaowed loudly at her. 'Alright, alright, it's dinner time for you,' she said, and led the cat into the kitchen. 'Would you like a tea?' she asked from there.

'Yes please,' I replied.

'Take a seat in the living room.' Once my coat was hanging up I walked into the neat little living room. I took that opportunity to look around the room and soak in what I could.

On a sideboard were a selection of framed photographs, one of which was a portrait of a muscular, athletic, blue-eyed man. I picked up the frame and looked into his eyes.

'That's my favourite photo of him,' said Heather, who had appeared in the doorway with a tray.

'When was this picture taken?'

'Earlier this year,' she said, putting the tray down on

the coffee table. 'I took it myself.'

He didn't look like me and I must say that the name Eugene didn't suit him. He was more of a George or an Alex but definitely not a Eugene.

Of course his face was not the one printed in the newspaper. Didn't she think that was odd?

She handed me a mug of pinky-brown tea.

'He doesn't look anything like he did in the paper,' I said.

'That was infuriating. I called the newspaper to try and get them to correct the mistake, to at least publish an apology but they refused. They just wouldn't listen to me.' She took the frame off me as though my time was up. 'He really was quite a mysterious person, I'm finding out. I didn't quite realise this when he was alive. His mother died a few years ago and he hasn't seen his father in over a decade so the funeral was a really small turnout. It was really me and my mother and brother, and a couple of friends of mine. That's why I was so surprised when you appeared at the grave today. Where did you say you knew him from?' I hadn't said.

'School,' I said, thinking quickly.

'You went to school in Hong Kong too?' *Hong Kong*?

'Only for a term,' I said. 'But even in that short time I made friends with him. He was just such a thoughtful and generous person.'

'Eugene, you're talking about? The last thing I'd describe him as is thoughtful and generous.'

'Why would you say that?'

'He was tight with his money and could be really selfish. He was convinced he struck people as a bit cold. But I saw the true him. I like to take credit for bringing

82

his caring side out of him. It was always there, he just needed to find someone who would take the time to look beyond the surface. And he cared for me deeply. I know he did.'

'I know exactly what you mean. I got to know the *real* him.' The silk of this web I was weaving was winding around me. I could feel myself starting to sweat.

'How did you end up becoming friends?'

'Well, you wouldn't believe this but we had the same name.'

'Your name is Eugene as well?'

'Not only that but my surname is also Blake.'

'Really?' She seemed to get excited by this, at least at first. But what was excitement turned to confusion a moment later. 'What's the likelihood of that?'

'Yes, I found it highly unlikely that he would have my name. If anything I was convinced he stole it from me.' She laughed a little. I didn't find it very funny.

She looked closely at the photo in her hand and I could see the longing in her eyes for a man who was never coming back.

But in *his* eyes I had seen a fraud, someone who had plucked my name out of the air and assumed my identity. It was now *my* face plastered all over the newspapers, not his. She didn't really know this man, this dead man who was going to be the future father of her baby.

I wanted an excuse to look around upstairs so I asked permission to use the bathroom.

I opened the bathroom cabinet and my eyes wandered across the creams and soaps and toothpaste tubes. My eye was caught by a pill bottle that had a prescription label with my name on it. I picked it up and looked more closely at the label. 'Eugene Blake. Memory pills. Take one a day. Do not exceed dosage.' Across the bottom was a logo that read 'Zarkoff, Inc.' This was the first time I had come across any evidence of this Zarkoff that the barber had told me about.

The bottle was almost empty with only three pills rattling around. I stuck it into my pocket and headed back downstairs.

Heather Blake looked decidedly more anxious than she had before I went upstairs.

'Who are you really?' she asked when I got back to the living room.

'Eugene Blake,' I said.

'I thought you looked familiar. *That's* where I know you from… the newspaper. You're from the newspaper! What are you up to?'

'I just want to straighten out this mix-up. I wanted to know who was buried in my grave.'

'But it's not your grave, it's Eugene's grave. The only mix up was that the newspaper put your face in the paper rather than Eugene's. Why did they even have your photo anyway?'

'I might have gone missing a while ago.'

'Missing?' she went silent. 'Did you ever really know my fiancé?' I could tell that she knew I didn't and had lied about knowing him. That also meant that I was standing in her home under false pretences.

'Get out,' she said, marching to the front door and pulling it open. The rain pounded hard outside. 'Get out now!' she yelled.

I grabbed my wet socks, picked up my shoes, and stepped out onto the doorstep. She slammed the door shut and I could hear all the locks being turned.

My socks were too wet to put back on so I stuffed them in my pocket and stuck my bare feet into those damp leather shoes and walked on out into the rain.

As I walked I gripped the bottle of pills in my fist. They seemed to hold a spell over me. It felt like it was offering up a clue as to what the other Eugene Blake had been wrapped up in. 'Eugene Blake. Memory pills. Take one a day. Do not exceed dosage'. I twisted off the safety cap and stared inside: three little pills looking up at me. I let one slip out into the palm of my hand.

I knew it was a bad idea but I thought that if I threw it into my mouth as quickly as I could then no one, not even I, would notice, and before I knew it it was too late: that pill was already slipping past my gullet and swimming down inside me.

Now I'd see what this was meant to do. I gave it a second to see if there was any instant reaction but I didn't feel any change. I closed the bottle, put it back in my pocket and kept walking.

A disappointment set in. I thought somehow these pills would reveal what it felt like to be the other Eugene Blake but instead I didn't feel very much at all. The name 'Memory pills' suggested that perhaps my memory would be enhanced, or that I would start to uncover long-lost memories that had been buried years ago. Maybe those memories would offer up a clue. Or maybe 'memory pills' suggested a transference of memories from the false Eugene Blake into my own brain. I would be able to see what he had seen, would see everything that lead up to his sitting down in that barber's chair and everything that lead up to his laughing fit. But instead not very much of anything happened and no clues presented themselves.

I had walked these streets a thousand times before but that night, for some reason, I was having trouble remembering exactly where I was going. I turned left where I should have turned right. I turned around where I should have gone straight ahead, and what should have been a half-an-hour walk turned into an hour's perambulation. If anything those memory pills hadn't helped one bit to sharpen up my memory.

Eventually I found a tube station and carefully followed the green line home.

It turned out I had been only a couple of stops away the entire time.

Chapter Fourteen

When I got out of the tube station I was struck hard by the shock of familiarity. The street leading away from the station was one I had walked hundreds of times and as my feet stepped over the pavement I realised how little I had appreciated the cracked paving stones and as I passed the huge supermarket with its overblown, functional architecture, I took back everything I had ever thought about it being a monstrosity. Instead this homecoming had revealed a beauty in its bleak facade, its orange colour scheme, and in trains of trolleys that snaked out through the empty car park. There was even a beauty to the walls of bottle banks.

And as I walked home everything held a fascination: the flashing orange spheres that bookended the zebra crossing; the iron fence that surrounded the park which had been heavily dented by an errant car's bumper; the telephone exchange box which had been left unlocked, with its spaghetti of cables spilling forth and its eerie, unnerving ticking; the foxes that stalked their way down the centre of the street when they thought that no one was looking; the newsagent that I'd never stepped into that stayed open until all hours of the night; even the lines in the road, the yellow 'Wait' box at the traffic light and the bank of cash machines held an interest. All these things were mine, they belonged to me, and soon I would be back home where I belonged and once I stepped through the door I would lock it and never leave my house again.

As I got closer to my block of flats a sense of urgency enveloped me and I found myself hurrying to the main entrance, punching in the keycode and ascending the internal staircase two steps at a time.

I had already fished my key out of my pocket and gripped it tight. I had kept hold of that key as though it were a precious metal and had carried it around wherever I went. When I missed home I would stare at its jagged edge; that little piece of metal represented the place I had always wanted to return to. And after months of reflection I had come to the conclusion that all I wanted was a quiet life, which is why when I heard the sound of metal ribbing into the lock I felt an astonishing sense of homecoming.

But between turning the key and pushing the door open my dreams were killed: the door stopped hard against the brass chain that was secured from the inside.

Confusion paralysed me. If I had the key how could the chain be on inside? Soon answers, though unclear, started to present themselves.

The wrinkled face of a worried woman appeared just beyond the chain. Blinking, troubled eyes, pin-pricked with fear, glared out at me. 'What do you want? Who are you?' she asked, her questions stabbing out at me in the dark.

'What are you doing in there?' I asked back.

'We've got nothing worth having.'

'Who are you?'

'You can't break in here. Go burgle someone else. Number 302 are much richer than us.'

'How could I be breaking in if I have the key?'

'That's our key!' she said.

'It is *not* your key. It's my key.'

'Go away or I'll call the police.'

'I'm the one who should be calling the police! You're in my flat!'

'This is *not* your flat!' I then heard another voice from behind the door, a man's voice.

'Who is it?' The woman's face disappeared and I heard her say:

'A tramp is trying to burgle us, Frank. Tell him to go away.'

'You call the police, I'll fight him off.' And now his face was in the gap. He didn't look happy. Even in the darkness his face glowed red. 'Go away!' he shouted and pushed at the door, whacking it against my foot. It served to both stop the door from closing and also really hurt my toe. I pushed back.

'I'm not going, this is my home. Where are all my things?' I asked, sliding my eye around the crack in the door to try and get a view inside.

'You're mad. You've got the wrong address.' He pushed the door so hard that he was at risk of have it come off its frame. It slammed shut and I banged hard against it.

I could hear doors opening elsewhere in the corridor but when I turned they slammed shut.

Inside I could hear the woman on the phone to the police.

'They'll be here soon,' shouted the man through the door, 'they're on their way.'

I instinctively knew my case didn't look strong. I was a dishevelled stranger banging on the door of an elderly couple in the middle of the night. I needed time to think.

And as I made it down to the front door I was shocked by how quickly the police had arrived. It was only a moment later and blue flashing lights were lighting up the courtyard.

I retreated the other way along the corridor and left through the service door at the back of the building. I snaked around the corner and watched as the officers approached the entrance and talked to the couple over the intercom. They quickly started to look around for me and that was all I needed to retreat. I found myself sneaking through the shadows away from the home I so desperately wanted to return to.

A hunger enveloped me as I walked the streets. I hadn't eaten all day and so when I saw a late-night newsagent's lit up at the end of the road I paused outside. There was fresh fruit on display outside and I looked over the apples, pears and nectarines. I picked up an apple and walked inside. The man behind the counter was half asleep and came to life when he heard me approaching.

As I walked away from the newsagent's I sunk my teeth into it and it turned out that this midnight apple was juicy and succulent and for its duration felt like the greatest apple I had ever eaten.

I spent the night wandering the streets and I eventually sat on a bench in the freezing cold. What I did there couldn't exactly be called sleep, more an upright drifting in and out of consciousness until five o'clock rolled around.

Chapter Fifteen

I returned to my home and stood outside like a stranger. I was itching to storm inside and demand they let me in but I knew that nothing good could come of that, and I was now toying with the idea of waiting until they left and just letting myself in. I couldn't decide whether I should confront those charlatans who had stolen my flat from me or wait until they had left and just let myself in. After all I still had the key.

But then I saw my old neighbour walk out of the apartment block, a man who had lived upstairs from me. Surely he would remember me.

'It's been a long time,' I said, approaching him. His eyes searched my face for any clues as to who I was. 'I live in the flat below you.' He was a little startled, which is probably how I would be if a man suddenly appeared from out behind a tree.

'You do?'

The problem was I couldn't remember his name. In fact, I didn't *know* his name. The entire reason for this was that I had never taken the time to find it out. I had seen him walking back and forth from the shops but I, in my self-centred view of my world, had never even said hello, had never stopped to chat, had never asked him how he was. And now I was about to ask him for help. But I could see he was struggling.

'Don't you remember? I'm from 110. I was away for a while but I'm back now. You should really come over some time. Do you like cake? I could get some cake.'

'Number 110? No, no, no,' he said, shaking his head, 'that's all wrong. Number 110 is Karen and Peter.'

'But how long have they been in there though? I was only away for six months.'

'How could you have been away for six months if they've been in there for longer?'

'That's not possible. They have not been in there longer.'

'They have. At least a year. Really nice couple. So neighbourly. They had me over for Christmas.'

'I'll have you over for Christmas.'

'But I don't know you.'

'We used to pass each other all the time.'

'Did you say hello?'

'No.'

'Then how do you expect me to remember you?'

'How come *I* can remember *you*? Don't you pay attention to the world around you?'

'I'm ninety-two. I gave up paying attention years ago.' He looked great for ninety-two, I must say. I would have said late eighties, tops.

'I need you to do me a favour,' I asked him.

'I'm not giving you any money.'

'Not money. I need you to verify that I live here. I need you to come up with me to number 110 and tell them that I was your neighbour and say that there's been a terrible error - an administrative and bureaucratic error - and that the flats have gotten all mixed up.'

'Absolutely not. I've heard of people like you, taking advantage of the vulnerable and infirm. Before I know it you'll be siphoning off my life savings. Now leave me alone.'

I stepped aside and let him pass. He really didn't seem to have any recollection of me living there and he had me wondering whether I had ever lived there at all.

I looked up at the block, at my flat itself, and wondered if I had got the building wrong. There were other buildings that looked similar to it, other blocks in the court.

And as I circled the block I wondered if I was in the wrong place completely. I mean, in that I was in the right place but also the wrong place. Maybe this flat was a reconstruction of my building, a perfect replica, but wasn't my building. But if the road leading to my building was the same then that meant that that road would have to have been a reconstruction too. And if that road was, then other roads had to be, all leading away from here. And how far would that go? While I was away had the whole city been reconstructed? Was I in an exact replica of London where I was a stranger, a total unknown, with no past at all?

I started to see everything in a new light, to look at buildings I had seen many times before and now saw nothing but fakes. The streets themselves, too, and the trees, and the very people walking around, all forgeries. I was the only one privy to this information. Everyone else was walking around in a false city and only I knew the truth, and I marvelled at the realism of it all, the convincing materials that everything had been made out of, and the exacting attention to detail. Everything was functional: all the door handles worked, all the cars ran, and the precision of it all was astounding. All the shop shelves were stacked, all the tills functioned, and everyone went about their day as though this was the real world. The roads were all positioned in relation to each other with perfect accuracy.

And I started to look up into the sky at the clouds and at the birds that passed by and I started to wonder if they were reconstructions too.

Chapter Sixteen

I had nowhere to go so I walked into my local library and sat on one of the chairs that were tucked into a secluded alcove at the end of one of the aisles. As I sat there in a fog of exhaustion from my lack of sleep from the previous night all I could think of was Zarkoff. And sitting there amongst all those books I started to wonder how many times his name appeared within this library. And I picked up a book and turned to its index. No entries. Then another book. Nothing.

I snaked around the stacks, seeing if there was a book that drew me to it, that quietly called out to me, that would contain the secret of who Zarkoff was.

Later that afternoon, after several further failed attempts I found myself with the UK business directory in my hand. And there I did find something: an entry for a Brian J. Zarkoff who had a business address listed.

I quickly wrote it down.

When I got there it turned out it was a funeral and embalming parlour at the dark end of a North London high street. The windows were frosted and I couldn't see any lights inside. The opening times suggested it should still be open, at least for the next fifteen minutes.

I pressed the buzzer hard and it made an ugly sound deep inside the building. I waited and thought I could hear faint signs of movement. Then the door opened sharply, spilling light onto the pavement, and a face stared out at me. The room was bright inside and the man looked at me expectantly.

'Yes?' he asked. He was holding a brown bread sandwich in his hand that he seemed eager to get back to.

'Is Zarkoff in?'

He nodded and waved me in.

I entered the reception of the softly-furnished parlour.

'Take a seat,' he said. 'Dad will be back soon.'

'Dad?'

'Yes. It's a family business.' Once he had taken a bite of his sandwich he said, mouth full, 'Oh, and I'm sorry for your loss.'

'Oh, no, it's nothing like that.'

I found myself sitting on the sofa and noticed the box of tissues on the coffee table. This did not seem like the office of a master criminal.

'Your name is Zarkoff, right? With a zed?' I asked him.

'It certainly is.'

Sitting there and waiting for Zarkoff I started to steel myself for confrontation. This was the man who had destroyed my life, who had bumped me off, and now I found my former life slipping through my fingers. I was about to meet a dangerous man, a man who could have you killed with one phone call, who probably has strings tied to all areas of the criminal underworld. I could feel my fists tightening in anticipation of a fight.

The front door opened and a man entered.

'Dad, this man is waiting for you.'

A frail-looking man turned to me. His head sprouted wispy white hair. 'Oh. I didn't realise. I'll be with you in just one minute,' he said, removing his green parka. 'Has my son offered you anything? A cup of tea?'

'Oh, no, that's all right,' I said, politely.

'Well, I'm sorry for your loss,' he said, clutching his coat. He hurried into the back office. After a moment he popped his head out. 'Please join me in here.'

I walked into his immaculately tidy office. As he hung his coat up on the back of his chair I made sure to shut the door. He sat down at his desk. 'Take a seat,' he said, gesturing to the chair in front of me.

'I'd rather stand,' I said.

'Okay,' he said. I stared at him rather than saying anything. I thought maybe he'd ask a question but nothing came out.

'Are you Zarkoff?' I asked.

'Yes.'

'Do you know who I am?' He shook his head. 'You haven't seen me in the paper?' He frowned a little, took a somewhat hard look at my face.

'The paper?'

I held his stare, trying to see what he was hiding behind those kindly, worried eyes.

'What are you hiding?' I asked.

'Hiding? Nothing.' In that moment I became certain that he was the man I had been looking for. This was not based on any evidence. I was just willing it to be true.

'Oh, come on,' I said, 'your secret's out.'

'What secret?'

'You know perfectly well who I am. What kind of

operation is it that you're running here?'

'Operation? We're a funeral parlour.'

'You mean you deal with death. I can't help feeling that there is something more sinister behind all this.'

'There is nothing sinister about death. We treat the dead with respect.'

'Well you didn't treat me with respect, did you?'

'You?'

'You probably had a body come in with my name on it, didn't you? Now there's some stranger buried in my grave.'

He looked at me in a new light, a look of fear. He rose from his desk.

'We are a legitimate business. I don't know what ideas you've got into your head but I'm going to have to ask you to leave,' he said, heading towards the door.

I don't know why I did it but I stood in front of him, blocked him from the door and stared into his eyes as menacingly as I could. He looked really scared and I instantly regretted doing it. I felt sorry for him.

The wave of shame and embarrassment was enough to propel me out of there and I hurried back through the reception and out onto the street. I walked as fast as I could.

Chapter Seventeen

I kept walking until the city gave way to the suburbs. Past midnight I was so tired that I just had to find somewhere to lie down. I snuck into some woodlands that overlooked a dual carriageway and lay down on the ground and from there I could hear the sounds of cars rushing by. Not even the sound of that late night traffic was enough to keep me from sleep.

For the next few nights that woodland became my home. Every day I emerged and walked to the local high street where I would eat my lunch and dinner, and returned every night to that spot. I had found a tarpaulin that had been discarded nearby and it came in useful. I fashioned a crude tent out of it and sat inside when it rained. To prevent it being pitch black in there I bought a small torch and found that inside my tarpaulin all my problems seemed to disappear. In the dim light I was no longer troubled by Zarkoff nor Maxwell, and I felt like my time as a private detective had just been in my imagination, that it hadn't really happened. Inside my tarpaulin the world did not bother me. It just left me alone. I had become invisible to the world.

At night the purple glow of the sky was the only clue that there was a city that lay beyond the woodland. I would sometimes forget I was in London entirely and instead start to believe I had somehow escaped. If it wasn't for the rushing cars on the dual carriageway I could convince myself I was entirely alone in the world.

During the day I would sit on the bank of the dual carriageway and observe the cars going by in the same way that someone else might watch the flow of a river. I wondered whether any of the drivers spotted the man sitting on the verge eating crisps and sausages sandwiches.

I caught myself in the reflection of a shop window and I realised how long it had been since I had seen myself. I found my reflection had somehow gotten mixed up with someone else's.

I did not recognise the man I saw. His clothes were tattered and blackened, his face grimy, his hair greasy and overgrown, and protruding from his face was a heavy beard. But most remarkably he looked *thin*. His newfound meagre diet was enough to transform him.

I could no longer accurately say I was who I thought I was. I felt like I no longer had any history, like my past had been erased. And without a past I therefore only existed in the present, existed only in the very thing I was doing at that time. But sometimes, when I was under that tarpaulin, I forgot to exist even in the present until it felt like I didn't exist at all. I had fallen through a crack in the city and found myself nowhere at all.

The sound of cars rushing past was a constant one. At all times of day and night I could hear that stream of vehicles and it was so relentless that my brain started to phase it out, to silence it, and what had kept me awake at night became comforting, became a sound that told me I was home. Some nights it even contained a lullaby. And one night while I was drifting in and out of sleep I could swear I could hear what sounded like a phone ringing without end. I was willing someone to pick up the receiver, to cut off that torturous sound so that I could fall asleep. Eventually it did stop and I was left with the rushing sound of cars and trucks careering along that endless stretch of tarmac.

But that ringing found its way into my dreams and when I woke up, with the sky bright and grey above me, I seemed to have brought that ringing back with me into the real world because there it was, somewhere in the distance and this time it did not stop, it just kept ringing on until it was all I could think about. I emerged from my tarpaulin to search for where it was coming from.

I headed towards the dual carriageway and as I did so the ringing became more distinctive, separating itself from the sound of the traffic. I stood on the edge of the verge and looked down towards the tarmac. It was only then that I spotted a phone, an emergency phone beside the crash barriers down below. That was where the ringing was coming from.

I stepped precariously on loose, dry earth towards the barrier, my feet slipping and skidding a couple of times, but I managed to make it down to the barrier without losing my step. Car horns honked as drivers were clearly alarmed to see someone heading towards the oncoming traffic.

The phone was still ringing as I reached it. I lifted the receiver, silencing it, and held it to my ear.

'Hello?' I asked.

'Why don't you answer your phone?' asked a voice.

'This is not my phone.'

'I heard you've been looking for me,' the voice said.

'Who is this?'

'You're Eugene Blake, aren't you?' I knew who it was a split second before he said it out loud. 'This is Zarkoff. I feel we've got to know each other so well already.'

'How did you find me?'

'You weren't too hard to find.' I looked around at the verge and the cars blurring past. I was surely in the middle of nowhere.

'Where are you?' I asked.

'I know you've been looking for me. How about we meet face to face? I can tell you everything you need to know once and for all.'

'When?'

'Today.'

'Where? What time?'

'At a hotel, in Soho.' He gave me an address and told me to meet him at four.

As soon as he had stopped talking he put the phone down and the line went dead.

I put down the receiver and started the arduous task of grappling my way back up the verge. Only once I had got to the top did I discover a concrete staircase only a little way along the road.

Part 3

Chapter Eighteen

When I arrived in Soho nothing seemed to be in the right place. Shops I remembered had disappeared and a cafe seemed to be on the wrong side of the road.

I stood across from the Regency Hotel and refrained from going in. I did not want to be the first to arrive. I would rather Zarkoff wait for me than wait for him.

I didn't see anyone go in or out but from where I was standing I could see a concierge through the window.

I let the minutes tick by but when he did not appear I convinced myself that he must have been waiting inside for me so I walked across the street and into the hotel.

Fumes hit me, a burning smell that saturated every inch of the air. I discovered a lobby with an entire wall that had been blackened by fire. The carpet in front of it had burnt away and the ceiling above was charred to a pitch black.

The concierge, who later introduced herself as Anna Boryova, saw that the damage had grabbed my attention.

'What happened here?' I asked.

'Just ignore that. We had a little accident last night in the downstairs kitchen.'

"A little accident?" Surely that was an understatement. Half the lobby was burnt to a crisp. I squinted and felt like I could see the haze of smoke still in the air. On the ground I noticed that the outline of a sofa had scorched itself into the exposed floorboards. 'Was anyone hurt?'

'Fortunately not,' she said.

'Do you have any idea what caused it?'

'They say it was the toaster.'

'The *toaster*?'

'It was a very expensive toaster, too. I really hope it doesn't cause you any inconvenience during your stay. As compensation we are offering free tea or coffee in our lounge. You are checking in today?' she asked.

'No, I'm just meeting someone here.'

'What is their name?'

'Zarkoff.'

'There is no one by that name staying here.'

'And no one's shown up in the last fifteen minutes?'

'You are the only person to have shown up all day. You are welcome to wait in our lounge. I can bring you a complimentary cup of tea if you'd like?'

I walked into the lounge which was really a stuffily-decorated front room that looked out onto the street. Thick green drapes hung over the windows and a heavy tartan pattern ran throughout the carpet. A sofa was positioned by the ornate fireplace and I sat there flicking through a wildlife photography book I picked up from the coffee table.

Anna Boryova brought through a cup of tea and set it down beside me and only once she had left did I notice its dark green colour. It was a herbal tea of some sort: a murky, thick concoction that I stirred around and tried to loosen up a bit. As it was a kindly gesture from a hotel I wasn't even staying in I felt obliged to sip it.

I put the piping hot water to my lips and sucked it in. It was strangely flavoured, surprisingly beefy for something so leafy. I tasted thyme in there, I think, and possibly rosemary. It was a curious-enough flavour that it made me want to keep sipping even though I couldn't say I enjoyed it.

As I browsed through photos of lions of the Serengeti exactly nothing happened: Zarkoff did not show up.

When I looked out of the window I did not see a single person pass by, and when I looked down at my watch I realised that the second hand had stopped ticking. It was frozen on sixteen minutes past four. I looked around for a clock but could not find one. For all I knew I had been sitting there for an hour.

I had started to become drowsy and had to battle my heavy eyelids. If I didn't get up now I would fall asleep on that sofa.

I slapped the book shut and set it back onto the table. I heaved myself off the sofa and walked back to the reception.

'It looks like he's not showing up,' I said to the concierge.

'Well would you like me to take your name and if he does show up I could tell him you stopped by?'

'That would be good. My name is Eugene Blake.' She had started writing it down but she stopped mid-word.

'*You're* Eugene Blake?'

'Yes,' I said.

'Your room has been ready all day.'

'My room?'

'Yes, your room,' she said, picking up a key from her desk. 'Here it is.'

'But I didn't book a room.'

'You did. I prepared it myself this morning.'

'There must be some mistake. I did *not* book a room.'

'I am absolutely positive you did. I think I even have the message right here,' she said. She turned and pressed a button on the answering machine.

'I'd like to book a room for next Wednesday,' said a voice. 'I'll be arriving at four fifteen. My name is Eugene Blake: B-L-A-K-E...'

To be fair, it did sound a lot like me.

'And if I remember correctly,' she said, 'you arrived at four fifteen and your name *is* Eugene Blake, isn't it? You just said so yourself.' That I couldn't deny. 'So by adding all of that up,' she said, dangling the key in front of me, 'the only conclusion can be that this is your room.'

I couldn't fault her logic and my brain was so tired that I was finding it hard to even attempt to counter her. Besides, I could use a lie down and the room would allow me to get some much-needed rest. Maybe after a little nap this whole thing would make much more sense to me and I could straighten it out then.

I took the key from her and headed up the stairs. The staircase was narrow, as was the whole building, a tall, skinny construction slotted between the two buildings either side.

The hotel itself was eerily quiet and fussily decorated: green, lightly-patterned wallpaper, maroon carpets and white corniced ceilings. Tired is a polite word for it. Totally knackered would be more accurate.

I put my key in the door but it refused to turn inside

of the lock. I took the key out and put it back in again, but it just refused to turn. And just as I had convinced myself that she had given me the wrong key I realised that I was on the wrong floor entirely. My room was on the floor above, directly above the locked room.

I reached my room on the next floor up, entered my key into the lock and turned. It produced a satisfying *click*.

Inside I found a compact hotel room: a single bed, a desk, a chair, a chest of drawers and a side table.

I locked the door behind me and looked out of the window at the view of a brick wall, so close that I felt I could reach out and touch it. Down below, a shadowy alleyway.

I tugged on the bouncy string in the small bathroom, shedding light on the bath, sink and toilet that had been slotted snugly together.

The fan whirred.

There I saw myself in the mirror. The only thing I recognised were the eyes. My beard was scraggly and hid a now-gaunt face. I turned on the tap and, using the disposable razor provided, proceeded to battle with my beard, scraping and scratching at it with that thin little blade until I could see flesh again and I kept going until that blade was blunted and the hair was no longer on my face but scattered around the sink. And once that was done I took all my clothes off and turned on the shower and scrubbed myself until all the dirt came off. I was washing off the earth I had been sleeping in, something I knew because I could see soil circling around the drain. I was starting to feel like a new man.

I wrapped the dressing gown around me and sat down on the bed which sagged under me with a drawn-out screech. I lay down on top of the covers and stared at the ceiling. Fatigue dragged my entire body deep into the mattress and there was nothing I could do to hold back the wave of sleep that washed over me.

Chapter Nineteen

I was awoken by a knock at the door, knuckles that rapped me out of my slumber. I flailed around on that sunken mattress as I tried to get back up onto my feet.

I eventually opened the door to find Anna Boryova holding a tray.

'Your breakfast, Mr. Blake,' she said, handing it to me.

'Breakfast? What time is it?'

'Ten o'clock.'

'At night?'

She frowned. 'No, morning. You must have really needed that sleep,' she said.

I took the breakfast from her and closed the door. The tray contained a small pot of coffee, scrambled eggs, bacon, sausages, and a rack of buttered toast triangles. I hadn't realised just how hungry I was but I sat at the desk and wolfed it down.

Later I tried to open the chest of drawers but the drawer did not budge. I pulled hard at the handle but I pulled so hard that the front of the drawer came off. It revealed that it was not a drawer at all but just a frontage stuck onto a thinly-constructed empty cabinet. What the hell was the point of that?

'How did you sleep, Mr. Blake?' asked Anna Boryova when I eventually headed down to the lobby.

'I don't remember,' I said. There had been hardly even a flicker of a dream to signal to me that I was sleeping. Instead there was a dead, blank nothingness, a block of lost time.

'I am going out for a walk,' I said, 'but I am still waiting for Mr. Zarkoff. I am expecting him to show up today but if he shows up while I'm out you must make sure he waits for me.'

'No problem,' she said. 'I'll make sure he waits for you.'

Chapter Twenty

When I stepped out of the hotel I found myself in the midst of Soho. Not that there were many people about. A few lone men walked up and down the street. The strange thing was that there were no cars at all: none parked on the street and none passing by.

A silence deadened the street. I could only hear traffic if I listened closely to the sound in the distance. I could not hear the sound of a single bird in the sky. Looking up, they were conspicuous by their absence.

I passed a cinema where a man in overalls was atop a ladder, clipping letters between the tracks on the marquee. So far it spelled out 'Film Noir Festi'. Posters hung outside with titles such as *Detour*, *Gun Crazy* and *The Stranger on the Third Floor*, each one more startling and lurid than the last. There were guns, *femme fatales* and promises such as 'The Most Explosive Picture You Will Ever See!'.

Next door I found a cafe and drifted inside. I sat at the counter and tapped my fingers on the bar. This place was empty too. No one behind the counter and not a single customer. I listened to the faint sound of rock and roll playing from the speakers and my eyes drifted around the sporting memorabilia on the wall. Behind glass were two boxing gloves and a small plaque claiming they had once belonged to Rocky Marciano.

A middle-aged man did eventually appear from the doorway behind the counter. He adjusted his apron and slipped on a little white boat-shaped hat which he slipped over his wispy hair. He seemed surprised to see me.

'Where did you come from?' he asked, as though I had materialised out of thin air. I could have asked him the same question.

'Are you open?' I asked. I thought maybe I had made a mistake.

'Of course we are open. We're always open.' He walked to the door and flipped the hanging cardboard sign from 'Closed' to 'Open'. I hadn't even noticed it on my way in.

He poured me a mug of black coffee without even asking for my order.

'Where is everybody?' I asked. He looked around at the empty chairs and tables.

'Everybody?'

'The other customers.'

'Oh, the *customers*. You're customer *numero uno*, the first lucky customer of the day.'

'Is it some kind of public holiday today?' I looked down at the date on my stopped watch.

'No, not that I'm aware. I guess its just not a good day for coffee.'

I picked up the jet-black coffee. It was so strong that I felt a wave of bitterness attack me before the cup had even reached my lips.

'Have you got any milk?' I asked.

'We're all out of milk,' he said.

Out of milk?

I took a sip. It was so strong that it obliterated my tastebuds. I struggled to swallow but eventually managed to gulp it down.

I slid the menu out from between a sugar pot and a ketchup bottle. All it said was:

<u>Sandwiches</u>

Ham
Cheese
Ham & Cheese
Chicken
Ham & Chicken
Chicken & Ham

All sandwiches £1.90

'One ham sandwich,' I said.

  'We're out of ham.'

  'Out of ham?'

  'Yes.'

I looked at the menu again.

  'Chicken then.'

  'Out of chicken too.'

'Here's an idea: why don't you tell me about what you *do* have?'

  'Do you like cheese?'

  'Sure,' I said.

'Then I will make you the best cheese sandwich you have ever had.'

  'Fine,' I said.

He disappeared out the back again and time stretched

out for so long that I started to wonder whether he had been a mirage. I was starting to forget what he looked like.

But when he did appear, sweatier than before, he planted a squashed white bread sandwich in front of me.

'*Et voila*,' he said.

It had been flattened within an inch of its life.

I looked from the sandwich to him and back again. He seemed to be watching me expectantly.

I raised the sandwich to my mouth and took a bite. I discovered the most buttery sandwich I had ever experienced: two slices of white bread drowning in butter and squashed either side of a single, thin slice of impossibly mild cheddar.

'How is it?' he asked.

'Excellent,' I said, lying as best I could as I suffered my way through it.

'More coffee?' he asked, picking up the pot.

'No!' I yelped, in a surprisingly high pitch, covering my hand over the mug.

Once both the plate and mug were empty he filed my coins away in the giant, clanking till and I headed back to the hotel.

Chapter Twenty-One

I found them in the bottom desk drawer: twelve empty notebooks, wirebound and lined. In the top drawer I found a bottle of ink and a fountain pen. I dipped the nib into the ink and sucked it up through the pen by winding the end. Since the pen was see-through the entire pen turned blue.

I found myself a new routine. I would sit down at eight o'clock every morning and put the nib against the page and I soon found that the pen took on a life of its own. It appeared as though it wanted to confess, to tell my story from the very beginning through to the very end. And I felt like I didn't have to make any effort at all. The pen did the work; I just had to hold it and let me guide it where it wanted to go.

At first it told nothing but the truth but what surprised me was how quickly the truth began to bend. It started with little white lies and veered towards overblown fiction.

Since I only had a finite amount of pages I wrote the words as densely as I could, using up every inch of paper and as I wrote I thought that I would at least leave behind a testament of what had happened to me.

Chapter Twenty-Two

It was only in passing that I noticed a little alleyway that ran down the side of the cinema. It led to a tall gate and when I pushed through it I found myself in an immaculately-kept garden. A little path wound around the flowers and trees and hedges, and at the back of the garden I found a bench.

I closed my eyes and tried to take in the natural world around me. I filled my lungs with air but it kicked off a coughing fit, as though inhaling the air was no good for me. I tried again but only managed half a breath before I coughed it back up. There was nothing fresh about the air. There was a thickness about it.

And that lack of freshness started to permeate through everything around me. My hand brushed the tall hedge that the bench backed onto and it felt synthetic. And as I looked closely at a patch of forget-me-nots I could not see a single insect on the soil below. No life of any kind. And the flowers looked so perfect, so vividly blue, that they almost seemed too good to be true.

I got up from the bench, placed my nose right up against the petals and took a deep breath. But there was no scent. The forget-me-nots smelled of nothing-at-all.

And I brushed the petals with my fingers and they felt man-made, and I ripped the head off and looked closely at it. Within the petals I could see fibres. I brushed my hand over the narcissi, the carnations and the hydrangeas and all of them were fake too. It seemed that nothing in that garden was real and I started to feel sick. There was a sickness in the air, a morbidity that permeated every inch of that garden. The idea of an artificial garden felt to me like a very sinister joke. I got out of there as quickly as I could.

Chapter Twenty-Three

'Is there something in the air?' I asked Anna Boryova when I returned to the hotel.

'What kind of something?'

'A lifelessness? A sickliness?'

She clearly didn't know what I was talking about.

'Are you okay?'

'I don't feel so well.'

'You don't look so well.'

'Did Zarkoff show up?'

'No,' she said.

'Okay, well, let me know as soon as he comes. I need to go to my room. If he shows up, knock on my door.'

'No problem at all,' she said, writing my instruction down on a hotel notepad.

I lay on my bed and felt the weight of fatigue come over me again. I didn't realise sleep would take over me so heavily because when I woke up it was dark outside. I quickly realised that I must have missed Zarkoff, and I hurried downstairs.

'Mr. Blake,' said the concierge as I approached her. 'You had a visitor.'

'A visitor?' I asked frantically.

'He said his name was Zarkoff.'

'Didn't you tell him to wait?'

'He said he couldn't.'

'Why didn't you wake me up?'

'He left you this note,' she said, handing me a piece of paper.

Dear Eugene,

I'm sorry to hear you are not feeling well. I am unable to come by tomorrow but I shall come by the day after and then we can finally talk, once and for all.

All the best,

Zarkoff

'Why didn't you knock on my door?' I asked, clearly exasperated.

'I did but there was no answer. You must have been in the deepest of sleeps.'

'But you know I've been waiting for him. You should have knocked harder.'

'I wouldn't worry, he will be back, just like his note says.'

I was annoyed she had so casually let him leave and hadn't even tried to get my attention. He was the only reason I was staying in this dingy hotel.

I headed across the road to the cafe and sat back down at the counter. 'Have you got anything other than cheese today?' I asked.

'You don't like cheese?'

'It's not that I don't like it, it's just that I'd like a bit of variety.'

'Don't worry, I'll make it good,' he said, putting on his apron.

'Is there a gents here?' I asked.

'Downstairs.'

I headed down to the basement and found the toilet. I clicked the switch outside the door but it had no effect. Luckily there was a square frosted window just above the cistern that let some light in. I squeezed into that little room and slid the door shut. As I stood there I could feel the sink press up against me on one side and the door pressed up against me on the other.

I stared at that little frosted window, a bright square of white light, and I started to wonder how it was so bright. Surely the cafe backed onto some buildings which meant that the square should really be in shadow.

By the time the toilet was flushing I had become so curious that I was tugging at the handle on that little window. It refused to move and I wondered if it had been painted over. I continued to pull on it and after some considerable effort the window snapped open.

Looking out through that little window from inside of this tiny toilet room I saw a field stretching out towards the horizon. There was grass and tall, bare trees reaching up into the sky and when I stuck my hand out the window I could feel the breeze against it. I stuck my face as close as I could to the window and I could feel the breeze on my face too.

There was a knock at the door.

'Is everything okay in there?' I heard.

'Yes, everything is fine,' I said, pulling the little window shut.

I slid open the door to find the owner standing there. He peered inside at the window and then at me.

'Your coffee is ready,' he said.

I sat at the counter sipping my coffee and every now and then looked at the owner and wondered whether he knew anything about that window. Had he ever looked through it?

The coffee was as bad as before but I was getting used to it. And there was something about that buttery sandwich that I had started to like.

Chapter Twenty-Four

I sat in my room and could feel the walls moving in around me. I'd been stuck in this little room all evening and couldn't take it anymore.

I grabbed my coat and headed out.

The light from the cinema marquee seemed to light the entire street and drew me to it. The words 'Film Noir Festival' beamed out up above.

I approached the box office, a little booth in which a bored girl had been trapped.

'How much for a ticket?'

'It's free.'

'Free? What's playing?'

'Old movies.'

'Which old movies?'

'I don't know. Look at the posters.'

'You can't recommend any to me?'

She shook her head. 'I haven't seen any of them. Movies aren't really my thing.'

I took the unnumbered ticket stub she gave me and when I walked into the cinema the film was already rolling. Faces loomed large up on the screen.

There were men dotted about here and there, plumes of smoke rising as they puffed on cigarettes in the dark.

I sat towards the front so that the screen enveloped my field of view.

The sound crackled and there were scratches all over the picture, a picture that jumped around the screen, with sound that popped and hissed. The film print looked like it had been dragged along the road and all the way into this cinema. It had probably been played a thousand times before.

I looked around and wondered if this cinema was usually used for adult movies. There was a dinginess about the place. The walls seemed to sweat all by themselves.

As I'd come in at the very end of the movie I had no idea what was going on except that the main character was in trouble and I found a man running through an alleyway and into the street where headlights exploded a beam across him. Wheels squealed into motion and soon sent his body flying over the car.

A guy in a white tuxedo got out and stepped towards the corpse. He flipped the body over only to find his eyes wide open and a gun pointed right at him. *Blam*!

The words 'The End' emblazoned themselves on the screen. These old movies really didn't wait around.

The light of the projector dimmed and they didn't even bother to take the house lights up. Instead a silence lingered and the smokers took this opportunity to let their coughs flare up and die down before the light of the projector started up again.

A logo came up - Monogram Pictures - and then a title. *The Electric Detective*. I couldn't believe it. Some unknown, square-jawed actor was playing Jack Claw and the movie opened in his detective's office. It didn't take long for a blonde to appear in the doorway.

'Come in,' he said. She walked in ghostly, all dressed in black. He let her glow in the light and he just played it cool.

'Cigarette?' he asked. He didn't wait for an answer, he just handed one to her and struck a match.

She proceeded to give him a sob story about the death of her husband. She'd just come straight from the funeral and she wanted him to do everything he could to find out who shot him. Because I'd read the book I knew hers was just an act.

The film deviated from the book quite a bit and soon the story had ricocheted off in another direction.

Later Claw was in white tie and sitting in a classy nightclub watching the widow, now dolled up in a sparkling silver dress, sing a number up on the stage, *All Dressed Up With a Broken Heart*. It went something like this:

All dressed up with a broken heart,
As beautiful as a work of art,
Don't know when my life will start,
I'm all dressed up with a broken heart

The climax of the movie came when Claw was locked in a study and he's doing everything he can to escape: he tries to break down the door, tries to pull up the floorboards, but then the room starts to fill with water. At first it just covers his feet, then it reaches his waist, and pretty soon its up to his neck. And just then, when the water was up over his head and he's gasping for air, the picture tore apart and only a beam of white light was left on the screen. Others at the back of the cinema started to grumble and I waited to see how Claw would get out of that one.

But when the projector started up it was another film entirely.

That was enough for me to walk out.

Chapter Twenty-Five

A subdued atmosphere filled the street and night had done nothing to liven it up. I spotted a bar across the road that streaked neon across the pavement.

I stepped inside and found men dotted around, nursing their drinks at the edges of that dimly-lit bar. The barman looked at me as though he had been expecting me all night.

He looked just like the guy who served me cheese sandwiches. When I stepped up to the bar I hesitated and looked him in the eye.

'Are you...?' I half-asked.

'Am I what?'

There was no sign of recognition in his eyes.

'Never mind,' I said.

There was only a single unmarked beer tap.

'A beer, I guess,' I said.

He poured the foamy beer into a heavily dimpled glass.

I stuck my hand into my pocket to pull out some money but he stopped me. 'No, that's okay. You can pay later. Just relax and take your time,' he said, handing me the beer.

I retreated to an empty booth, sat down and took

several long sips, sucking it down within me, and only when I stopped for breath did it hit me. It was a smoky, hoppy, punchy concoction like nothing I had had before and once the wave of flavour had flown through me I put it back to my lips again and proceeded to gulp down the rest.

'Another?' asked the barman when I reappeared.

'Yeah,' I said. 'Another.'

He brought it over to me this time and when I gulped from it I found that the novelty failed to wear off. It still felt like a great new discovery and before I knew it I was on a third.

'What do you call this stuff?' I asked.

'It doesn't have a name. We make it ourselves.'

It was on the fourth that I started to float, or maybe the room started to sink, but that wasn't enough for me to reject the offer of a fifth. I savoured it, trying not to gulp it down too quickly, but it was during the sixth when I started to lose count. I did not know if the sixth was the fifth or the fifth was the sixth. I frankly don't remember how many I had.

In fact I don't remember very much of anything.

It was only later, the next morning - no, the next *afternoon* - once I had awoken in my hotel room, that some memories of that bar seeped their way through the cracks. Answers about what had happened the night before came from Anna Boryova. She told me I appeared in the doorway and just passed out on the floor of the lobby. She couldn't well leave me there so she had to ask a passerby to help her drag me up the stairs. She said it wasn't far off having to move a piano.

I was barely functioning, just a dead weight in bed waiting for life to return to me.

I went back to bed only to wake up in the middle of the night. I had missed the entire evening.

Lying in the darkness of my room I could have sworn I heard two voices. I wearily got out of bed and looked out of the window into the alleyway but there was no one to be seen. It sounded more like it was coming from inside the building, which meant that there must have been other guests staying somewhere in the hotel.

I put my ear to the wall but it did not reveal anything. I then got down onto the floor and put my head to the carpet. The voices became more pronounced but the floor was still enough to muffle exactly what they were saying. I think that somehow through the carpet, underlay, plaster and light fixtures, I heard them say my name.

Now that I was awake I discovered an intense hunger inside of me. I hadn't eaten all day and my stomach cried out so loudly I could actually hear it.

I was forced to put some clothes on and go find something. As I was getting dressed I could hear those voices again and they only became more pronounced once I walked downstairs. It felt clear to me that they were coming from the guest room below mine, the one I had accidentally tried to unlock when I had first arrived. But very soon after I had put my ear to the door the voices stopped and only silence remained.

I walked through the empty lobby and out onto the street only to find that most of the street was dark. But up on the corner a newsagent's was illuminated and spilling light out onto the pavement.

Out the front fruit had been laid out and the apples, pears and nectarines offered up a colourful array in the otherwise monochromatic street. I picked up an apple but it was far lighter than it should have been and I instantly knew that it was plastic. And I touched the other fruit: the oranges, the bananas, the peaches, all plastic too.

I took the plastic apple inside with me.

The storekeeper had his chin balanced on his hand, his eyes shut. He was falling asleep.

'Excuse me,' I said. His eyes flashed open.
'What do you want?' he asked sternly. It wasn't exactly traditional customer service.

'Your fruit…' I said.

'What about them?'

'There's something wrong with them.'

'You don't like them?'

'It's not that I don't like them, it's just that they're plastic,' I said, holding up the apple.

'Let me see,' he said, holding out his hand. I handed him the apple and he threw it across the room where it bounced on the tiled floor and rolled under a refrigerator. 'We're all out of apples.'

There was a silence as though that explained it all and no further details were required.

'What about the oranges? They're plastic too.'

'They are?'

'Are you all out of those too?'

'Must be.'

'And the bananas and the pineapples?'

'All out.'

'Do you have any real fruit in here at all?' He just stared at me. 'If you're out of fruit why not just admit it? Why stock your shelves with fakes?'

'Well, our shop would be empty then, wouldn't it?'

'Do you sell anything real at all?' I asked, reaching

131

for a box of cereal on a nearby shelf. It too was light and when I tore it open I found that it was totally empty. As was the box next to it. And the box next to that. 'These are totally empty!'

He shook his head and tutted as though it were just a big shame. 'We must be out of those too.'

'But you're not out of them, are you? You've still got the boxes,' I said, swiping the shelf and letting the boxes tumble to the floor.

'That's seriously impolite, man,' he said, coming out from behind the counter and picking them up.

'Do you have any actual food products in here at all?' I picked up a chocolate from the counter and opened it only to find it had been stuffed with polystyrene.

I started to step towards the door, startled by the madness of a shop that didn't actually sell any products. As I stepped back over the threshold I lost my footing on the front step and knocked into the fruit stall, sending the plastic apples bouncing into the street.

I ran back to the hotel, through the dark reception and up to my room. I locked the door behind me, took off my clothes and jumped into bed. I pulled the duvet over my head and shut my eyes tightly.

I pleaded for sleep to grab me, to drag me down into the depths, and in that darkness I saw my old flat and ached for home.

Chapter Twenty-Six

When I awoke the next morning I was drenched in sweat and had to peel myself off the mattress. The moment I stood up a wooziness forced me to grab the desk. If I hadn't I most certainly would have hit the carpet.

I slowly put on my clothes and as I headed for the lobby the stairs seemed to warp under my feet.

I must have looked terrible because Anna Boryova was staring at me wide-eyed.

'Is everything all right?' she asked.

'I'm not feeling so good,' I said. 'I think I need a doctor.'

'There's one just down the street,' she said, picking up the phone and making an appointment. When she put the phone down I asked her:

'Are there any other guests staying in this hotel?'

'You are our only guest, Mr. Blake.'

'That's strange because I heard two voices from the room below mine. Are you sure no one else is staying here?'

'The room below yours... no, that room is empty. There's no one staying there.'

'Okay,' I said. Maybe I had just imagined the voices.

She took me outside and pointed to the end of the road. She was right: the doctor's was remarkably close, and only a moment later I was walking into the reception.

The waiting room was empty. Drops dripped from the ceiling into a bucket and a damp patch had taken over so much of one wall that it had saturated the medical posters on the noticeboard.

'I have an appointment,' I told the receptionist.

She took a long look at me.

'Doctor Montgomery will see you. Room 1C.' She looked back at her computer screen.

'And where is 1C?' I asked.

She pointed, flinging one arm out in the direction of the corridor behind me. I walked along, found door 1C and when I knocked I heard a voice instruct me: 'Come in!'

The office was a mess. Files and papers covered every inch of the doctor's desk and spilled onto the floor. Up above, a lighting panel flickered. A bookcase was stuffed two rows deep with medical books. Standing in the corner, pressed up against the bookcase, was a model of a skeleton that was now being used as a coat stand. And from behind those stacks of paper I saw the doctor's white hair. He looked up; a pair of thick-rimmed glasses stared out at me, eyes slightly magnified.

'Mr. Blake, please, come in, sit down. I won't be a minute,' he said. He stared at his computer screen.

The chair was covered in papers. I picked up the pile and put them down with everything else on the floor.

'Please excuse the mess. I'm currently in the process of getting all this paper typed up into here,' he said, tapping the side of his computer monitor. 'It's taking a little longer than I had hoped for.'

He sighed, pushed the keyboard away from him and gave me his full attention.

'Now, what seems to be troubling you?'

'I'm having a crisis,' I said.

'A crisis?'

'Nothing feels real anymore.'

'I see.'

'I mean, everything looks real. I'm *here*,' I said, tapping my arm. 'I know that much, but there's a chest of drawers in my hotel room...'

'A chest of drawers?'

'Yes... when I pulled out the drawer, it just came off and revealed the chest was hollow. I mean, why would a hotel just have something that looks like a chest of drawers and not actually *be* a chest of drawers?'

'I don't quite follow.'

'That's just an example. Have you been to the grocer's at the end of the street?'

'No, I haven't,' he said, shaking his head.

'They're selling *plastic fruit*,' I whispered, as though it were a secret.

'Plastic fruit? That used to be quite popular. For decoration. We used to have a bowl on our dining table years ago.'

'No, not for decoration, to *eat*.'

'You can't eat plastic fruit. It would play havoc with your digestive tract.'

'Have you ever heard of a grocer's selling plastic fruit? I've never heard of that before.'

'Are you sure it was plastic?'

'It's not just the food that doesn't seem real around

here. I found a garden where every leaf, every petal, is man-made. There is not an inch of real life in there. And... and...' It felt cathartic to be able to finally articulate what it was I had been feeling. 'And where have all the birds gone? And not only the birds but the *people*. Where is everybody?'

'You mean you're experiencing a sense of loneliness?'

'No, that's not it at all. I'm not lonely, I'm alone! Sometimes I feel like I'm the only person in the world.'

He scribbled something down on a notepad.

'It is possible that when someone is so caught up with their own problems, for example an intense loneliness, it can manifest itself in the real world. Your mind *chooses* not to notice the people around you.'

'And what about the air? It's so thick and stale. Don't you feel it too? Sometimes I feel it's difficult to breath.'

'You're having difficulty breathing?'

'I have difficulty finding fresh air.' He took out a stethoscope and pressed it against my back. He asked me to take deep breaths.

'Do you have any difficulty breathing now?'

'Not right now,' I said.

'I see. Say "Ahhh",' he said and stuck a tongue depressor in my mouth.

That was followed by a torch drifting from one eye to another. He took my blood pressure, recorded my height. The tests culminated in him measuring the width of my head with a calliper.

'Is this really necessary?' I asked.

'I'm afraid it is, for a man in your condition.'

'My condition?'

He did not feel the need to elaborate.

With a tape measure he recorded the length of my arms and legs and I felt like I was being fitted for a suit rather than undergoing a medical examination.

He sat down back down again.

'I just have to get all this information in here,' he said, tapping on his keyboard.

'Is that going to take a long time?' I asked.

'No, not at all.' Except it did take a long time. He pecked at the keyboard with one finger for what seemed like forever. 'Now all I have to do,' he said, once he had finally finished, 'is hit return, and…'

He whacked the Return key and the sound of a printer whirred up beside him. Once the perforated paper had been churned out he tore it off and examined it. 'Oh…' he said.

'Is "Oh" bad?'

He picked up the phone and rotated his chair away from me, stretching the curly cord.

'We've got a case of a four-one-three here…' he said. He was whispering, speaking conspiratorially. But I could hear every word. 'Yes, I thought so too… okay…' he said. He found himself wound up in the telephone cord. He rotated himself back until he had been freed and replaced the receiver.

'Is anything wrong?' I asked.

'Something's come up in your results. It's the software, you see. We enter the data and the computer prints out the diagnosis.'

'What does it say?'

'Nothing serious. It just says that you need further testing.'

'Further testing?'

'Yes. It is important to attack these things early.'

'What things?'

'It's nothing to worry about. I just need you to take all your clothes off and put on this robe,' he said, picking up a blue gown that had been draped over a stack of books behind him.

'Now?'

'Yes, now,' he said. 'You can go behind the screen,' he said, pointing at a curtain.

I pulled the curtain back and stepped inside. I took off all my clothes and put the robe on. When I swished the curtain aside he was gone.

'Doctor?' I asked.

The door opened and he appeared in the crack.

'Follow me,' he said. I walked in my bare feet along the corridor to a room a few doors down.

When the door opened I found a small lab with all kinds of machines installed around the room. A musical combination of buzzes, beeps and whirrs played out quietly in the background. A young man with bushy hair and bad skin was standing in the corner in a white coat. He did not introduce himself.

He picked up a chair and brought it to the centre of the room.

Doctor Montgomery sat on the chair and filled in a form on a clipboard.

'Surname?'

'You know my name.'

'*Surname*,' he repeated, seriously. I resigned myself to participating in the formalities. 'Blake.'

'Forename?'

'Eugene.'

'Middle initial?'

'H.'

'Now we're just going to perform a few tests,' he said, which seemed to activate the assistant. He turned out the lights, leaving only an eyesight chart illuminated.

I read out letters from across the room. 'E... F... P... T... O... Z... L... P... E... D...'

The assistant then stuck a pair of headphones on my head and had me listen for a beeping sound that pulsed softly. I was to press a button whenever I heard it.

That went on for a long time and I clearly missed a few at the start but by the end of it felt I had pretty much mastered it.

'Okay, you can take the headset off now.'

'What's the result? How's my hearing?'

They didn't answer me as though it was their hearing that needed testing.

They then tested my reactions, setting me in front of a machine that flashed a red light at me. Every time it flashed I had to press a red button. I pretty much mastered that, too.

'We will now be testing your cognitive abilities,' said the doctor, presenting me with a written test. 'You have two hours.' And with that the doctor and his assistant started to leave the room.

'Wait... what?' I said.

'I'll be back when your time is up,' he said, and they left me alone in the room with the test paper sitting on the table in front of me.

I flipped open the paper and looked at the first question:

Write 6.3×10^{-2} as an ordinary number.

What the hell?

I leafed through the rest of the test and it had the heft of a small book. Each page contained complicated mathematical problems.

The wall ahead of me was mirrored so when I looked up all I saw was my baffled face staring back at me.

I picked up the pencil and after noodling over the first question I moved onto the second:

Mr. and Mrs. Brown buy tickets to see the butterfly sanctuary for themselves and their four children. The cost of an adult ticket is £8 more than the cost of a child ticket. The total cost of the six tickets is £68. What is the cost of an adult ticket?

For a moment I thought I had the answer but my mind fogged. The rusty cogs of my brain whirred wearily and I eventually got something down on the page. I pushed through, distracting my wandering mind with doodles around the margins, and I wasn't too far from the end when Dr. Montgomery came back in and announced 'Your time is up.'

'Thank God for that,' I said.

He sat at the table and proceeded to mark the test with a red pen he removed from his jacket pocket. His wrist was flicking so wildly that I couldn't discern a tick from a cross.

He closed the paper, wrote a number on the front, and pushed it towards me.

Twenty-three percent.

I was happy with that.

'Not good,' he said.

'I was amazed I got anything at all. You should have been pleased I even completed it.'

'You didn't complete it. You left twelve pages blank.'

'What is this actually supposed to prove?'

'It proves that we're going to have to perform further tests.'

'What's next? GCSE French?'

He handed me two pills and a little cup of water.

'What are these?'

'You may feel a little drowsy after these but that is perfectly natural.'

'Drowsy? What's this for?'

'For your brain. To sharpen you up.'

I looked at the two little pills in my hand before popping them into my mouth and swallowing them with water.

'If you'd excuse me for a moment, I'll fetch your results from the next room.'

'More results?' I asked.

He left me alone and I looked at myself in the mirror. I couldn't help feeling I was being watched.

When he returned he held a short stack of papers and a folder in his hand.

'We need to have a little talk,' he said. 'You might have a little problem.' He put his papers down on the table and took a seat. 'You no longer exist.'

'Excuse me?'

'We have created a new identity for you. You now have a new name, new papers, and a new history. We have an apartment waiting for you.'

'What are you talking about?'

'Pretty soon you will not remember that Eugene Blake ever existed.'

'How?'

'The pills. The memory pills. Not to make you remember but to make you forget. You will now transition between your old and new life. You will leave here a new man.'

'I just came here to see a GP because I was feeling out of sorts. I am ready to go home.'

'You are, are you?'

'Yes.'

'Back to your old life?'

'Yes. Back to my old life where I was happy.'

'How can you be so sure of that, especially when you wanted to be here?'

'I never wanted to be here. I was tricked into coming here.'

'You came here under your own free will. There was no trick involved. In fact, you pleaded, you begged to be inducted into our programme.'

'What programme?'

'We have all the documentation to prove that coming here was your decision.'

'What are you talking about?'

From the file on his desk he pulled out a piece of paper. The first thing I noticed was the letterhead: Zarkoff, Inc.

My eyes snapped to him.

'*You're* Zarkoff?' I asked.

He shook his head. 'Just a representative.'

'A representative? Of what?'

My eyes scanned the page.

I hereby authorise Zarkoff, Inc. to submit me to the medical procedures outlined below and from here on out I hand over all ownership of my name, my likeness and my history. I do not hold Zarkoff, Inc. responsible for any loss of identity…

'Loss of identity?'

'That is what you came to us for.'

'What do you mean?'

'To get rid of Eugene Blake.'

I think by that point I was starting to find it difficult to remember just who exactly Eugene Blake was. I couldn't help but feel that Eugene Blake was already going a little out of focus.

'But here,' I said, 'it's signed by Eugene Blake.'

'Eugene Blake himself,' he said.

Down at the bottom of the page was a signature. I couldn't be sure if that was mine or not.

'Do you not recognise your own signature?'

'I didn't come to you.'

'Well then if it wasn't you then who was it?'

'Look, there was an imposter out there, someone pretending to be me, going around telling people he was Eugene Blake. He stole my identity and now, I fear, I have been mistaken for him.'

'How do you come up with this stuff?'

'It's true. I have evidence. There was an article in the newspaper a few weeks ago. "Missing Man Laughs to Death in Barber's Chair" was the headline and now there is a tombstone sitting in a cemetery with my name on it. You can see it for yourself.'

'You know about the grave?' he asked. It dawned on me that he knew about it too. 'Well, that article, I'm afraid we might have put that article in the paper.'

'You?'

'Well, we didn't write it but it may have something to do with us. You see, in signing this document you gave up your name and your likeness and by doing so you allowed us to recycle your identity as we see fit.'

'*Recycle* my identity?'

'Yes. The man who died, by all intents and purposes, was Eugene Blake at the moment of his death. The real question is whether he actually died or not.'

'Of course he did. He was buried.'

'I wouldn't be so sure.'

'What do you mean?'

'Were you there for the burial? Did you see it for yourself?'

'No.'

'Did you see what was in the coffin?'

'No.'

'Then how do you know who - or what - was in there?'

'Look, I want to cancel this, whatever this is. Where's the cancellation policy?' I asked, flipping over the contract.

'Do you not remember why you came to us? You were in trouble, deep trouble. Something about you being a detective in over your head.' I remembered something about being a detective.

'It was a mistake. Whatever I said was a mistake.'

'I'm afraid the process is already underway. If we stop here it could result in some serious mental distortion. It could effectively split you in two. You have to see the whole thing through. That is the surest option.'

I snatched the contract from the desk and tore it in two. 'Now we have no agreement. You have to let me go.'

I got up and grabbed the door handle. It was locked. I slammed on the door. 'It's okay,' he said, as though he were talking to someone else, someone who must have been listening, and I heard the door unlock. The assistant was standing on the other side.

'Mr. Blake will be checking out today. Please return his clothes to him. He is free to go.'

I quickly changed into my clothes, marched through the waiting room, out onto the street and back to my hotel. I was determined to get out of there, to pack everything up and get back to my old life.

There was only one reason to return to the hotel: the notebooks. Looking back, I should have left them behind but at that point they felt like the only link left to my past, the only record of what had happened to me. But once I had packed the notebooks in my bag and headed for the door something stopped me. I couldn't bring myself to reach out for the handle, couldn't take a single step further. A fear had taken over me.

I felt that if I took one step over the threshold I would fall into an abyss on the other side. I had a distinct sensation that there was nothing beyond that door.

Instead I locked it, unpacked the notebooks, and started to write. I felt like my time was running out to record what had happened to me and I wrote for days on end. At some point there was a knock on the door.

'Is everything all right, Mr. Blake?'

I approached the locked door.

'Yes, everything is fine,' I said, calling through.

'Do you know how long you will be staying with us?'

'Date unknown,' I said. I wrote on into the night.

I wanted to tell my whole story, to document everything that happened. Maybe someone else would be able to make sense out of it. I found myself going right back to the beginning, to where this whole mess started. *My bones were a mess. Imagine a fat man - a really fat man - covered from head to toe in plaster with two sad little eyes peering out.* Maybe I wasn't *completely* covered in Plaster of Paris but in memory I was mummified. And when I walked into that charity shop, perhaps the raincoat wasn't in the window but buried in the rack and perhaps when I tried it on it wasn't the very first one I'd tried but rather I had tried on every raincoat I could find. Maybe I had been watching stacks of videotapes of old movies, had started to see myself as a hardboiled figure walking through London in the rain. But I wasn't that at all. Instead I was a lonely man in spongy trainers stepping into puddles. Only in memory was there a romance about it, perhaps distorted, but it was this romance that went down onto the page.

I don't want to make it seem like none of what I wrote was true. The facts were largely concrete, undeniable, but perhaps there was a slant to it, a romantic, fictitious slant to the whole thing. Fact dressed up as fiction. Or fiction dressed up as fact.

But I *did* find that first case, did meet Melissa White, and she did send me on the trail of her missing husband. That much is true.

Perhaps it wasn't quite a car pulled out of a lake. Maybe I saw that somewhere and it stuck in my mind. Maybe it was just a body in a field, and maybe she didn't quite recognise him as her husband, but it's just that the car coming out of the water was more engaging, more visual, and I thought it would be more exciting for the reader.

Perhaps I overstated my heroism and my athletic prowess. Perhaps I wasn't tied up in David White's basement and perhaps there was never a freezer, let alone a body, but there was indeed a car chase. Perhaps *high-speed* isn't quite accurate but there was a low-speed chase at least. And my car didn't quite fly through the air, and the world didn't quite spin into a knot, but my life did flash before my eyes like they said it would in all those stories. And then there was the crash. Perhaps not as dramatic as I made it out but the car did crunch against a tree, and perhaps David White didn't roast in a ball of flames but he definitely did not survive. At least that was what I was told.

I did return to my old life and the boredom crept in again. And this was my terrible affliction: boredom. It felt like a disease I had been born with and it infected my entire life. What I should have done is learn to deal with it, to embrace the boredom. Then I would never have been so compelled to escape. I had convinced myself that it was my job that was causing the boredom but I have come to realise that I had brought it with me. I unpacked the boredom at the beginning of the day and packed it up again at the end.

That was until I had that lightning-bulb moment, that hare-brained scheme, to become a private detective. Who else concludes that that is the very best solution to their problems? I realise now that I should have focused my attention on attaining an ordinary life, not an extraordinary one.

When the saga of my first case was over it was as though none of it had ever happened. Boredom returned as it had before and I couldn't remember the sensations, the fear and the pain I had felt, while I was working on that case. And my mistake was to not learn from my experience and to take on another case. I wasn't even looking for a case but the case of Jessica Palmer came out of nowhere and I found myself sleuthing again. My problem was that I wasn't thinking. When I started seeing Emily I could not differentiate the fact from fiction. If I had looked closer, if I had thought about it for one moment, I would have seen that it was all too good to be true. Why would a woman like her have gone for a guy like me? I was too sucked in by the possibility of it all. My imagination had gotten the better of me, as it always had and sometimes I feared that my imagination had become a substitute for reality.

Which led me to my current predicament. Had I completely been consumed by my imagination? Was there not a trace of reality left? All I could try and do was piece it all together in these notebooks, one sentence after the other, one word after the next, and hope that reality would rise to the surface somewhere on the page.

I had no idea how much time was passing. Was it hours? Was it days? Was it weeks? All I had to go on was the beard that had appeared on my face in the mirror.

I was so engrossed in those pages that I hadn't noticed the black smoke that was making its way under the door. It was only once the room was almost entirely filled that I ran to the door and pulled it open. The corridor was ablaze with a heat so intense that I felt I would melt if I left the door open for any longer. I ran to the window and pulled up the pane.

Directly below my window was the hard tarmac of the alleyway.

I stuffed the notebooks inside my bag and threw it out of the window and I stuck one leg over the window frame. I thought that was a good place to start. Now straddling the window, black smoke streaming over me, I leant my head out to try and catch a gulp of clean air. Soon after getting my other leg out of the building I found myself hanging by my fingers. Things weren't going so well. I could see myself falling through the air rather than feel it.

A blackout. For how long, I'm not sure.

I found myself on the tarmac. Pain shot through my body in so many places it was hard to tell where exactly I had been hurt, but I was at least able to pick myself up and retrieve my bag.

Streams of smoke billowed out of my little room on the second floor.

As I limped out of the alleyway it was the intense heat that stopped me in my tracks; it seemed to transmit pain effortlessly through the air. And at that moment I saw that all the buildings along one side of the street were consumed by flames: the front of my hotel, the bar, the cinema, all roaring red.

Only then did I realise the enormity of it all. Flames in the distance told me that the entire city of London was on fire.

The buildings were giving way easily. The cinema had caved in on itself, the marquee in fragments on the pavement, and the bar's roof had collapsed.

I hurried away from the flames as fast as I could but when I turned the corner I found that the next street was also on fire. I could see trees ablaze in the square in the distance and smoke was collecting in the sky, creating a rainless, menacing cloud up above the buildings. I was witnessing an entire city in the process of being razed to the ground and it really did look like the end of the world.

I turned another corner and found that construction work had created a huge barricade. There was no way out. I was only just discovering that I had been trapped all along and that there had been no way out even if I had tried to leave.

Time was now running out. The sky was filling with thick black smoke and my instincts kicked in. I only had one idea as to how I could escape.

I ran back to the cafe. It's upper storeys were smoking but I was able to get through the front door. I ran down into the basement and into the bathroom. I pulled open that little window and shoved my bag through.

I then went through after it.

I fell onto wet, grassy earth.

I hadn't noticed the rain coming down on my face and I grabbed my bag and ran as far away from the building as I could. And when I turned I did not see a city. Instead I saw a huge structure, as large as an aeroplane hanger, up in flames. And dotted around the field were people watching the devastating spectacle unfold, each one of them lit up by the glowing orange flames that reached towards sky. They had all escaped too, and I thought I saw the concierge and the bartender and the doctor amongst them. But I did not stay long enough to find out if it was really them.

And as I heard sirens in the distance I walked off into the night.

I found a road that was flanked by large houses and I kept walking until I discovered a small high street and there, on a map by a church, I found out that I was not in London at all but in a little village somewhere to the north. I made my way to the train station.

The carriage was empty and I sat at the back and when I looked out into the darkness all I could see was my own reflection. The world outside was really just a series of dotted lights but I at least sensed the space and land out there. I was returning to the real world.

The buildings of London came into view: streets and shops and stations and houses. There was something particularly convincing about them and I realised that what had been missing during all that time was a true sense of reality. Nothing had felt real and that was only too clear now that I was being subsumed by the city again. I could already sense the glass and brick and concrete. This was more like it. This felt authentic.

I wanted to re-experience the city as soon as I could.

As the train doors opened and I stepped down onto the platform I realised I was gripped by the people, by the sounds of the station and by the shops and kiosks around me. Everything felt so real. When I left the station a dark city revealed itself and I inhaled that cold, soothing night deep into my lungs. There were taxis and buses and people pushing past me. And they didn't care about me. They didn't care who I was. And that was the way it was supposed to be. That was the way I liked it.

Chapter Twenty-Seven

I found myself sitting on the steps of Eros and pulled my coat in close to me. A chill blew through Piccadilly Circus. Tourists were dotted around, taking pictures of each other. I imagined them unknowingly pasting images of me, the lone man somewhere in the background, into their photo albums. I tried to formulate a plan but my brain was too weak and my body too exhausted.

It got to half nine and I knew I couldn't just sit there all night. I would have to just keep moving.

I walked along Shaftesbury Avenue and passed the lights of the theatres. I then turned up Frith Street and absorbed the machinations of a living, breathing city. The espresso bar was busy, filled with night owls, partygoers and coffee dwellers. I wandered in and felt like I was right back where I had escaped from just hours before.

It was different inside. The sporting memorabilia had been replaced by movie memorabilia: Rocky Marciano's boxing gloves had been swapped for a portrait of Marcello Mastroianni.

I headed downstairs into the bathroom, sliding the door shut behind me.

There it was, the same little window. I grabbed it and slid it open. But instead of a field I saw the brick wall of the building opposite.

I walked up to the iron fence that surrounded the park at the centre of Soho Square only to find a lock on the gate.

I walked all sides of the square before coming up to St. Patrick's Church. The door was open.

Inside was quiet except for the sound of breathing. I discovered men, lying on the pews, fast asleep. Everywhere I looked I found another. The church was full of them. I took a seat on a pew and there I found my eyelids drooping and my head nodding until I was drifting in and out of sleep. But I fought it. I didn't want to give myself up so easily and count myself among the destitute of the city.

Around midnight it was raining heavily and I found myself on familiar territory, standing outside the barbershop where Eugene Blake, the *other* Eugene Blake, was found dead. And there inside, the lights still on, was the barber. He was sitting, eating a sandwich, and reading a paper, as though he were just waiting for a customer. The 'Closed' sign was on but I knocked on the glass anyway.

He put his sandwich down and approached the door, unlocked it and opened it ajar.

'Can I help you?'

'I need to talk to you,' I said.

He thought about it for a second and then opened the door wider.

'Come in,' he said. I stepped over the threshold.

'Take a seat,' he said. I took a seat in the gleaming,

red leather barber's chair.

He approached me, his reflection speaking to mine.

'You really need a haircut,' he said. He was right. I looked at myself in the mirror. My hair was thick; my beard, overgrown.

'Don't you recognise me?' I asked.

He looked me over.

'I never forget a face,' he said.

'I don't look familiar to you?'

'Afraid not.' He had already raised his scissors and started clipping.

'Maybe my name will be familiar to you.' He did not say a thing, just kept snipping away. 'Eugene Blake,' I said.

'That is not possible,' he said, matter-of-factly.

'And why not?' I asked.

'Because Eugene Blake is dead.'

'And how can you be so sure?'

'Because I saw his final moment with my own eyes.'

'And what if that wasn't Eugene Blake?'

'What do you mean?'

'What if it was an imposter?'

'Like an impersonator?'

'I'd say more of a thief, a man who had stolen Eugene Blake's identity.'

'But that cannot be. It was all in the paper in black and white. See?' he said, pointing to the wall. And there it was, framed proudly above the hair wax and barbercide. 'That article made me famous. The amount of people who come in here and ask me about that mysterious man who died in this very barber's chair... I think the morbidly curious just wanted to sit in the chair where another man died.'

He took out the clippers and set them buzzing. He pushed them through my hair, running paths along my scalp. And as he continued to do so, I started to realise that he was in the process of removing every hair from my head. And as I watched him do it I couldn't help but find it funny. There was something absurd about it. And then it started. It was a mere nasal exhalation at first but it quickly progressed to a vibration in my throat before turning into an open-mouthed hee-haw. I was buckled over in the chair, slapping my thigh, my eyes watering. Laughter had taken me over so extremely that I could no longer breathe. Then the laughter became locked inside and it started to burn deep within my chest.

The barber started to step back, unnerved by the spectacle occurring in front of him. And I thought that maybe this was the end, that I would never inhale again, and as the room faded around me I feared that I would prove it was entirely possible to die laughing.

Part Four

Chapter Twenty-Eight

The men of The Armchair Detective Society of Kent (and its surrounding areas) sat enthralled as Christina told them the strange story of how she had found Eugene Blake and what had happened to him. But just as the story was getting interesting, just as Eugene had escaped from the fire and was sitting on a train to London, a slide appeared on the screen with the words 'The End' on it, a phrase so resolutely final that it caused mild outrage.

'That can't be the end!' said Harry. Jimmy whacked him on the arm.

A ripple of applause travelled across the room and as the final claps faded out Bill took it upon himself to say, rather loudly, 'That doesn't make any sense.'

The others turned to him. They might have been thinking the same thing themselves but they weren't as rude as Bill.

'Do you have a question?' asked Christina, who hadn't quite heard what he had said.

'I'm just saying it doesn't make any sense. I mean, how could anyone be made to think they were someone else?'

'Yeah, I didn't get that part,' said Jimmy. 'Did you

explain that?'

Christina was worried that someone would bring that up. She had clues as to how it had happened but she had not yet been able to make any final conclusions about what she had found.

'I have a few clues as to how it was achieved. I believe it was some kind of brainwashing process.'

'And you say it was some kind of aeroplane hanger? What do you mean, it was all constructed out in the country somewhere?'

'I have not been able to locate it yet but I think I'm close to pinpointing where it is.' That was news to me. 'Think of it as a kind of movie set, a reconstruction of what seemed to be London but it was all a copy, a fake. But certain things could not be reproduced. It seemed to lack other people. And no birds in the sky. I guess what they couldn't reproduce was nature. It was a poor reproduction of real life.'

'I think there is far too much information missing,' said Bill.

'Well, that is what part two is for,' said Christina.

'Part two?'

'Yes. I shall return once I have more information and I can assure you that all will be revealed.'

'And how do you plan to get this further information?' he asked.

'I have a new resource that I'm hoping will be able to provide me with more answers. He also happens to be our guest for this evening.' And that was when Christina pointed to me.

I was standing in the darkness at the back of the room. I had been late and had to sneak in while the presentation was going on. Nobody had seen me come in and now all eyes were on me. I was kind of hoping Christina wouldn't point me out. I had hoped to sneak away before the lights went up but now I could see everyone itching to ask me questions. But I didn't expect the applause they gave me.

'Have a beer,' said Harry, cracking open a bottle.

'How did they convince you?' asked Bill, almost immediately. I was hoping they wouldn't ask that.

'I'm afraid Eugene will not be taking questions. He does not have all the answers himself,' said Christina.

'Things are still coming to me every day,' I said. 'I'm hoping to have a fuller picture soon.'

'And hopefully Eugene will return with me for part two,' added Christina.

I drank a beer with Harry and the men on the whole respected Christina's request but when they strayed into interrogative territory I just told them I couldn't remember very much. But when their curiosity became too much for them, and they started to crowd around me, Christina had to come to the rescue.

We made our excuses and said our goodbyes, and walked to the bus stop together through that cool night.

It was then that she told me.

'I think I've found it,' she said.

'Oh,' I said.

'And I think you should come with me.'

'I don't know if that would be such a good idea.'

I thought it over for a couple of days, tormented by the question of whether it would undo all the progress I had made. But a couple of days later I was sitting on a train with Christina heading out of London, reversing the journey that had been my escape. I wasn't at all sure if that was the right thing to do.

Chapter Twenty-Nine

Piece by piece, in flashes and in waves, it came back to me: how it had all started, how I had gone to them for help and how I had signed my whole life away. When I woke up on the floor of my living room, bruised and bloody, I knew what I had to do. It was as though Maxwell's punches had knocked the idea into my head and by the time I regained consciousness and opened my eyes the idea was fully formed.

I had never forgotten Alter Ego, the company that had helped David White disappear, that made it appear as though he had actually died. When his car was pulled from the lake they had even found a way to stick a body inside. And while I never wanted to do away with myself I thought that disappearing would be my way out.

Looking back on it this was a double disappearance. First I had become a private detective in order to escape my mundane life and now I was disappearing again by becoming another person entirely.

I went to see them without an appointment, just let myself in to their first floor Soho office. When the receptionist saw me there was a flash of recognition. Seeing as my face was all beaten up this was an impressive feat.

'Do I know you from somewhere?' she asked me.

'Is he in there?' I asked, pointing to his office and not waiting for an answer.

'You need an appoint...'

I pushed the door open and found him inside sitting behind his desk. He took my presence in his stride and did not look alarmed.

'I tried to stop him,' said the receptionist.

'That's quite alright,' he said, screwing the lid of his pen back on and setting it down on his desk. 'You can close the door.'

She did not look happy about it but returned to the reception and shut the door behind her.

'Do you remember me?' I asked.

'Of course I do, Mr. Blake. I never forget a face even though it doesn't look like yours is doing so well. Take a seat,' he said. I sat across the desk from him. 'You caused me quite a bit of trouble, you know.'

'I did?'

'Oh yes, a lot of trouble. That messy affair with David White, that horrible ending he had. I had quite a few questions to answer. I know you were involved in all that but there was nothing they could find to connect me to the case. It was just all a tragic accident. But I must say I never thought I'd see you again.'

'I need...'

'Wait, let me guess,' he said, interrupting me. 'You need me to help you vanish.' He pointed at me. 'Your face gives you away. I'm sure whoever did that to you got great satisfaction. You know, I've daydreamed about doing the very same thing to you. He saved me the trouble.'

'Can you do it or not?'

'What level are you thinking? We can help you lie low for a couple of months, or we can...' I picked up the briefcase and put it on the table. 'What's this?' he asked. He opened the case and looked inside. Even the sight of cash wasn't enough to surprise him. 'You *must* be in some trouble. I shouldn't ask where all this came from.' The money must have jogged his memory. 'I think I know what might work for you. We have a pilot scheme going on, something at the cutting edge. I think it will be perfect for you. They will give you an entirely new identity and you won't have to worry about your old one.'

'What does that mean?'

'It means that you can look to the future and forget about your past. You will be a new man.'

At that point it felt like my only option. 'I'll do it,' I said.

'Perfect. Wait here and I'll get the paperwork ready for you.' He left the room and I sat in that quiet room, my heart pounding.

He came back with the papers. 'Have a read through,' he said, handing me the contract, 'and if you're happy with it I'll just need you to date and sign it.' He unscrewed his pen and handed it to me. My eyes scanned the page.

I hereby authorise Zarkoff, Inc. to submit me to the medical procedures outlined below and from here on out I hand over all ownership of my name, my likeness and my history. I do not hold Zarkoff, Inc. responsible for any loss of identity that may occur during this process.

* * *

I didn't even wait until my eyes had reached the bottom of the page. I put the nib against the paper and scrawled my name across it.

'Perfect,' he said. This is yours,' he said, pushing a small bottle of pills towards me.

'What's this?'

'Take two twice a day.'

'What for?'

'It's step one of your new programme.'

He got up and opened the door for me.

'When do I start?'

'They'll be in touch.'

'Who will?'

'You'll find out soon enough,' he said.

As I was leaving, walking down the stairs to the street, I took a closer look at the label of the bottle. 'Zarkoff, Inc.'

I unscrewed the top, swallowed two pills, and screwed it back on.

Chapter Thirty

We took the train together and during the journey Christina told me how she had managed to locate the facility.

'After what I read in your notebooks I was certain that a fire on that scale could not just go unnoticed so I scoured the newspapers for any sign of a major fire this year. None of the big newspapers printed a single word about it but it was only once I had gone through all the local papers that I found it, a mysterious blaze about an hour outside of London. When I called the local council they were tight-lipped about it, claimed they couldn't tell me very much, but it seemed as though they just didn't want to tell. But from the maps I studied I figured out where the site must be.'

'So you're not certain where it is?'

'Well, we'll find out when we get there.'

The train pulled into the station an hour later and Christina looked closely at the map she had brought with her. We walked away from the picturesque village that we found ourselves in.

'I think it's this way,' said Christina, who would stop every now and then to study the map. 'It's only a little further,' she promised several times. I did not realise it was going to take us an hour's walk only to find ourselves standing at the edge of a field. It sloped downward towards an industrial estate surrounded by wire fencing. 'This must be it,' she said, and our shoes sunk into the mud as we walked towards it. Not a single blade of grass had survived the tyre tracks that had powered over them and as we approached the fence I didn't think there was any way we would be able to get inside.

'There's CCTV,' I said, and pointed to a camera that pointed right back at me. But Christina was not put off. She continued to walk around the perimeter.

The construction was several storeys high, cobbled together with sheets of corrugated iron. Container offices were dotted around the outside, some stacked two on top of each other. It looked so unremarkable in the grey daylight.

There were signs of fire damage everywhere, blackened areas where the iron was scorched.

'I can't see anyone here,' she said. 'Perhaps it's deserted.'

'Or perhaps they're watching us.'

'Does any of this seem familiar to you?' It looked so different in the light of day. It just looked so *ordinary*. Christina went off to explore.

I stood looking up at the building and wondered whether what I had experienced, a city which had seemed so expansive, could possibly have been contained within this sprawling and ramshackle structure that stood before me. And I felt a frustration that I would never see what was inside.

But I soon saw Christina walking towards me on the other side of the fence.

'They can't be watching this place too closely,' she said, holding up a padlock.

'You *picked the lock*?'

'Hardly. This thing was hanging open. Practically came off in my hands.'

I found and walked through the open gate, but the next problem we were faced with were more padlocks, bolted shut this time: huge, rusty things that would probably struggle to come undone even if we had brought bolt cutters with us.

We tried to peer through windows only to find that they were so dirty that they were almost impossible to see through.

Christina tugged at one of the bolted doors, clearly frustrated that we would not be making our way inside. But I had an idea.

'Come with me,' I said. 'There might be a way in.'

Christina followed me as I walked around the building.

And there it was: a small, square window. I approached it and grabbed the frame with both hands. And when I tugged it snapped right open.

Darkness inside.

Christina rummaged around in her rucksack and pulled out two torches. She flicked hers on and shone it into that little bathroom. 'You go first,' she said. She was smaller than me, much smaller, but I went in head first, which was probably not such a good idea, because I found my head coming dangerously close to the toilet below. I clambered down onto it and rolled onto the floor and, because there was no space in there, rolled out the door onto my back.

'Are you okay?' called Christina after me.

'Yes, all good,' I said, as I struggled to get back on my feet. And with the elegance of a gymnast Christina stepped easily inside and was soon standing above me holding out her hand. She pulled me up.

'How did you know this window would be open?' she asked.

'That's how I escaped.'

The stench of the burnt city had scorched a deathly smell into the air. And as I climbed the stairs each step creaked and I questioned whether they would collapse under my weight. I entered the cafe, a place I never thought I would step foot into again, a place that I had almost convinced myself had come to me in a dream, but here it was, that place from my dreams, anchored by reality. And although the cafe had partly survived the front wall was completely charred with a deep blackening running up across the ceiling.

The sporting memorabilia went from relatively unscarred to completely destroyed. Rocky Marciano's boxing gloves had transformed into two black blobs, and all the glass from the large front window had been smashed. The shards crunched beneath my soles.

I ignored the doorway entirely and instead just stepped through the window and out onto the street.

And as I shone the torchlight along one side of the street and then the other I saw an apocalyptic sight: a city burnt to a crisp.

Christina's torchlight emerged from the cafe and lit up the space next to me as she approached.

'What the hell is this place?' she asked.

'This is where I spent weeks of my life thinking it was the real world.' The thing was it now didn't look very much like the real world at all. In its blackened state I found it hard to imagine how I had ever thought it was real. It all looked too much like a set.

I shone the light back through the cafe. 'This is where I would come and sit at the bar and eat cheese sandwiches. It was the only food I could find in this place. There was a guy who would make them for me and we'd talk a little, but not very much. I wonder who he was, who he really was. I wonder what happened to him.'

We stood in the centre of the road and looked up at the buildings on either side. Now they looked like cut-outs, like plywood frontages rather than brick and mortar. Across the road was the cinema, its marquee lying on the ground, the announcement of 'Film Noir Festival' staring up at us in fragments, the letters scattered. I walked up to the door of the cinema and pushed it open. Christina followed me inside.

I shone my light up towards the screen to find no screen at all, just an empty space where the fabric once was. The light of my torch moved across the seats of the auditorium and towards the little square at the back of the room where the circle of the projector's lens could be seen.

I found the door to the projection booth, just off from the entrance. We ascended the steep iron ladder.

Christina and I looked around at the large film canisters stacked on the ground. One stack had the title printed clearly on the side of each canister: 'The Electric Detective'. I pulled off the lid of the upper-most reel - Reel 7 - and found the tightly-wound 35mm film inside. I pulled at the film leader and unwound a few feet. Shining the torch through I could see the little images running along the strip of celluloid: a man in a hat and raincoat walking through the pouring rain.

'What is that?' asked Christina.

'Just some old movie,' I said, and let it go.

We walked out of the cinema and walked up to the Regency Hotel. The front wall had burnt away and the blackened lobby could be seen from the street.

'This is it,' I said to Christina. 'This is where I stayed.' Her eyes passed slowly across the building and I could see her wondering how I could have bought it, how I could have not seen the hotel to be, like every building along this street, a facade. Perhaps the mind had played tricks. Perhaps I was under some kind of spell. Perhaps it was just convincing enough to allow my imagination to do the rest.

Christina was about to step inside but I instead led her to the back of the building. 'There, up there,' I said, pointing my torch up towards the window, still wide open. And passing the beam from the window to the ground I was shocked by just how far I had fallen.

'Was that your room?'

'Yes, that was it, up on the second floor.'

I wondered if the staircase had held out, whether it was even possible to get up there.

We returned to the street and stepped inside the ravaged lobby. Only a nightmarish version of the reception desk remained. I pressed one foot on the first step of the staircase and it seemed to hold. The second step too. Each step moaned under my weight but I made it to the first landing, then to the second.

When I stepped inside my room I found myself inside sitting at the desk, writing in my notebook, oblivious to the intruders and to the blackened room around me. When I looked to Christina I could see that she couldn't see what I saw and when I looked back I glimpsed myself falling from window, leaving behind the empty, hollowed out room. The bed was reduced to its metal frame and the desk had blackened.

The room was smaller than I remembered it, all its furniture crammed together. 'This is where you lived?'

'Yes,' I said.

'It's so small,' she said. 'I don't know how someone could live in a space so small.' The floor seemed to creak as though it were breathing under us.

'There's one final thing I'd like to check,' I said.

One floor down I slammed against the locked door until the lock gave way and the door swung open.

Inside I did not find the guest room I was expecting. Instead I found an office. In the place of a bed and a wardrobe were desks. It looked like it had been cleared out. Computer cables were strewn and melted on the floor but the computers they had been hooked up to were gone. The desks were empty. I looked up to the ceiling, up towards where I had been sleeping. Had I been surveilled? Had my every move been tracked? At that moment I felt certain that they had even found a way of recording the dreams of the man who slept above them.

I no longer wanted to be there. I could no longer understand why I had returned to the very place I had desperately wanted to escape from.

'I think we should go now,' I said, and we walked back down through the lobby, across the road to the cafe, down the stairs and back out through that little window.

As we walked across the field I did everything I could to prevent myself from looking back.

Chapter Thirty-One

I had truly believed I was Stanley Black. I had not questioned that fact. But ever since Christina had first said the name Eugene to me it kept popping into my mind at inopportune times. I found myself saying it out loud, just to hear what it sounded like. I wanted to know what it felt like to say. I would roll it around in my mouth like a sweet. And it started to fit. I would stare into the mirror, look closely at my face, and repeat the name to myself until there was no longer a disjuncture between the face and the name. They melded together until they just made sense.

I remember sitting in my living room at night. I was looking around the bare walls and listening intently to the silence around me, and I started to understand that this was not my home at all. I could feel myself hollowing out and becoming anonymous.

This new hollow state made it very difficult to sleep. I would stare at the ceiling until the early hours wondering whose bed I was in and trying to recall who I was before. In the darkness I could see snatches of an old life, little details in the dark. I had a sense of another room entirely: a bed, a sofa, a kitchen, all empty, waiting for my return. And I saw a woman, hazy to me, and wondered whether she was waiting for me. Or was my mind playing tricks on me in the darkness?

And this lack of sleep really started to derail my working days. Terry, my boss, was not happy with me showing up late and while I was working I would be totally distracted. Walking the streets I would feel a sense of anonymity, as though all the history and experience that had made up who I was had disintegrated, and this sensation followed me to work.

And then my job at the butcher's came to an abrupt end. Terry had not been happy with how the week had gone. I had been late every day since Monday and he told me that I had to be on time on Friday without fail. He was going to be late that morning as he had a family emergency and he needed me to open the shop alone. It was *essential* I arrived at seven to get everything ready for nine.

But when he came into work that day he found that nothing was ready. He found the door locked and the shop untouched from the night before. The butcher's was dark and the window display was empty. And it was ten a.m., a full three hours since I was meant to have shown up.

And I wish I could tell you that I was fast asleep, that I had missed my alarm and slept on into the morning, but, no, I was wide awake. I was sitting at my kitchen table, locked in a state of inertia. I was contemplating why I should be doing the work of another man. If I wasn't Stanley Black then why should I be doing his job?

At that little kitchen table I had come to the firm conclusion that I was indeed Eugene Blake and that I had to continue on as him. I had to shove a stake through the heart of Stanley Black, to sabotage his life, and have him reduced to dust.

Christina delivered the notebooks to me at my request and as I read them it felt like the story was being drawn out from somewhere deep inside me.

And while reading, a block of flats started to build itself in my mind, and from clues in the notebooks I started to piece together the location of where I used to live. The next morning I travelled across the city on the District Line and after some wrong turns found myself standing in front of a building that felt so familiar to me that I knew it was where I belonged.

I failed to get access to my old flat but discovered that the flat directly beneath mine had become vacant.

The moment I was shown around by the estate agent the familiarity of it hit me: it felt like I was home again.

The flat was identical to my old flat above it, one stacked on top of the other. The only difference, I was told, was that this flat had the original fireplace whereas my old flat had a blank wall.

'Does it work?' I asked the estate agent.

He had no idea.

I recreated my old flat exactly: I ensured that the walls were the same colour and re-bought the same old furniture and placed everything just where they used to be. And once everything was in place I had the uncanny sensation of homecoming. I felt as though that I had never taken this detour, that I had never become Stanley Black, and that I had always been Eugene Blake.

But one night I wondered if it would be better if my desk was up against the window. I pushed my bed across the room so that it now pointed inwards and then relocated my desk. Something felt right about this set-up, familiar even.

It was only once the flat was dark and I was heading to bed that night that I realised why it had felt so familiar. I could now see that I had arranged my bedroom to mirror the hotel room I had been trapped in.

The stacks of notebooks were illuminated by a patch of moonlight that had fallen upon my desk. I approached the notebooks, sat down and opened the first book...

My bones were a mess. Imagine a fat man - a really fat man - covered from head to toe in plaster...

...and I tore the first page out of the book, ripped it into little pieces, allowed those scraps to fall through my fingers and watched them drift to the floor.

I did the same with the second page.

I managed to get the coal alight and once the fire was flickering I threw the notebooks into the fireplace and watched with a kind of morbid fascination as the pages fought, then succumbed to, those flames: they browned then shrivelled then blackened.

It felt as though the fire was freeing me from the past and I watched until the paper had totally disintegrated and they could no longer be described as notebooks at all.

The next morning Christina arrived.

'Breakfast time,' she said.

I had totally forgotten that I had invited Christina round, or, more accurately, that she had invited herself round. There had been something important she wanted to talk to me about.

'I've got us coffee and croissants,' she said, which perked me up. 'What's that smell?' she asked, sniffing at the air. 'Did you have a bonfire in here or something?'

'I was just testing out the fire last night.'

She laid the coffee and croissants out in to the living room and we sat on the sofa.

'There's something I want to ask you,' she said, tearing off a piece of pastry.

'Yes?' I asked.

'I need your permission.'

'Permission for what?'

'To publish your story.'

'Publish it?'

'As a book.'

'Who'd write it?'

'You've already written it.'

'I have?' I asked.

'The notebooks,' she said. 'You wrote it down in the notebooks.'

I started to feel weird inside. My eyes flicked to the ashes in the fireplace then back to Christina.

'But I don't have them,' I said.

'Yeah you do. I gave them to you, remember?'

I did remember.

'I don't have them anymore.'

'Why not? Where are they?' she asked, biting into the croissant.

'I burnt them.'

She stopped chewing, her eyes locked on mine.

'You burnt them?' she asked, her mouth full.

'Yeah…' I said. 'The bonfire smell…'

Her eyes widened and she jumped off the sofa and

hurried to the fireplace. She brushed at the ashes and dragged out a curly wire that had held one of the notebooks together.

'I'm really sorry,' I said. 'I don't know what I was thinking.'

She looked up at me, in shock, but then, out of nowhere, began to laugh.

'What's so funny?' She tried to respond but was laughing so hard she could barely speak.

'The notebooks…' she said, 'I made copies.'

'Copies?'

'I typed them all up to keep them safe. It took ages.' I fell back on the sofa in relief. 'So I have your permission to publish them?' she asked.

'Yes,' I said. 'You have my permission.'

'I'll punch up some of the language,' she said, standing up, 'clarify things that don't make sense. You'd still be credited as the author. I'd just kind of be a ghost writer, that's all.'

Christina went to work on it immediately. It took up all of her time and I hardly heard from her for a few weeks. And then the day came when she presented it to me, three stacks of paper. The first manuscript she called *The Fat Detective*, the second *The Fat Detective in Love* and the third *The Fat Detective Disappears*.

When I got round to reading them I found out that she had rewritten a lot of the text. She had changed the names and obscured the locations; time was compressed, details were disguised. But her writing was far more vivid and delicate than the matter-of-fact prose I had scribbled onto those pages. It was a vast improvement on the originals that you read.

* * *

Six months later I was walking down the high road and saw it in the window for the first time. Morning light was streaming through the glass and cut across the cover. *The Fat Detective* by Eugene Blake and Christina Walker.

I walked inside the empty bookshop and picked up a copy from the table at the front. I took it over to the woman working behind the counter.

'Is this a popular one?' I asked her, holding it up.

'Not really,' she said.

'Have you read it?'

'Yeah, I have. I didn't much care for the main character and it was a bit too odd in places for my liking.'

I put the book back on the pile and walked out, vowing to never return to that bookshop.

I felt a distinct sense of achievement and only a few doors down I came across a new ice cream parlour that purported to sell the most genuine gelato this side of Italy. Even thought it was only ten in the morning I felt I had a reason to celebrate.

I looked down over the different colours looking up at me and I wondered which flavour would best fulfil me at that very moment. My eyes passed over the cookies and cream, the pistachio, the mint choc chip, the stracciatella…

Once the books were published something happened that I had not anticipated. It was only a few days later when the first one came in: am email dropped into my inbox, an urgent request for my attention. *I have a case only you can solve, a mystery that desperately needs looking into.* Before I had barely even composed a response to that email another appeared. *Please help me - I don't know who else to turn to.* This kicked off a barrage of requests from strangers for my investigative services.

I wrote a reply to that very first email, requesting further information to determine whether it was a case I wanted to take on but as my cursor hovered over the Send button I let go of the mouse and sat back. This was a world I had to stay out of, a world I could not let myself be dragged back into. I deleted my reply and glanced one last time at the queue of emails in my inbox before shutting down my computer and pulling out the plug at the wall.

I could see the snow coming down outside my window and it drew me out. I put on my boots, a fleece-lined parka and a pair of thick winter gloves. I stepped outside and drifted through the snow, letting the flakes settle on my coat. I walked past the cafes and shops as the light turned towards evening and it was at that moment that I saw it.

My raincoat was on proud display in the charity shop window. I had handed it in a week earlier and I felt like I was standing back in front of the shop where I had first found it, before I had ever made the decision to become a private detective. And it felt like I was being given another opportunity to make that fateful mistake again. I knew that my old raincoat was all I needed to take on those new cases. But I also knew that it had only brought me trouble. I had been shot at, beaten up and trapped. I decided then and there that I was going to have to resign myself to the experience of an ordinary life. No more missing persons, no more sleuthing. I would have to find a way to embrace the tedium of the everyday.

But you should know by now that I have a severe problem with will power and I found myself standing back outside the shop as the shop assistant re-dressed the mannequin with a fleece-lined parka. I tightened the belt on my old raincoat, pulled up the collar, and walked on through the snowy city.

christianhayes.co.uk

Manufactured by Amazon.ca
Bolton, ON

17248213R00101